To Megan, for being absolutely invaluable to me on a daily basis. You are the sunshine in my life, so here's a grumpy/sunshine for you. Thank you for always being a bright spot.

Chapter One:
The Note

Callie

I wake with a pounding headache, my eyes refusing to open as I roll onto my back and groan. Why the hell did I get that drunk? There honestly wasn't any legitimate reason for me to get fucked up on a Thursday, but here we are... wait, where are we exactly? *Oh fuck, please don't tell me I hooked up with anyone.* Only a creep would sleep with a girl that inebriated, and if that's what happened, I'm going back to that bar to slap the security guy.

He's a creep too if he allowed me to leave with some asshole.

Keeping my eyes shut, I take a mental check of my body. It doesn't hurt —

the night cap

okay, actually it does, but not in the places that scream sex. More like I fell a couple times instead. My vagina feels intact. I'm not restrained or held captive. I'm simply surrounded by the faint smell of whiskey, cinnamon and the most intoxicating scent that can only be described as *man*.

Shit. I definitely went home with a guy.

I sigh as I peek my eyes open, knowing with all of me it isn't any of my brothers' houses. None of them smell this good. I don't hear anyone else, so I sit up and swing my legs over the edge of the mattress to get a better look at the studio apartment. I'm in a king-sized bed with only one pillow, staring at a black leather couch, a kitchen that looks like it's never been used, a giant tv, and a floor-to-ceiling shelf filled to the brim with old records.

It's a bachelor pad, but easily I can tell this isn't some young guy's house. This one belongs to someone well accustomed to living alone and taking care of all his own crap. There's something endearing about that, knowing drunk me at least had some semblance of standards.

jensen

Don't talk too soon, Callie. You haven't seen his face yet.

Next to me is a nightstand with only the bare necessities on top of it, which makes the note lying next to a water bottle stand out like it doesn't belong. He's an alarm clock and lamp kinda guy. No way he leaves random notes with scribbles on them, so my nosey self snatches it up to read it:

RELAX, I DIDN'T KIDNAP YOU. FOR THE RECORD, I HAD NOTHING TO DO WITH YOU TAKING YOUR PANTS OFF. YOU YELLED "PANTS ARE FOR BITCHES" AND FELL OVER TRYING TO GET THEM PAST YOUR ANKLES. I'M HONESTLY A LITTLE IMPRESSED YOU SUCCEEDED.

KEYS ARE ON THE TABLE. DON'T PET THE DOG.

Dog? What dog? Another sweep of the room doesn't reveal any dog, but him telling me not to pet the thing has me worried. Will he bite me? Shit, I need to get out of here. I spot my keys on the kitchen table like he said, then grab the sealed bottle of water to chug a little too much before making a move to stand.

the night cap

It's then I meet said dog.

He's lying on the floor near the bed, and I didn't even notice him with how he blended in with the dark rug, but now he's looking at me and I would bet my Volvo I've never seen a grumpier dog in my entire life. "Nice puppy." I swear he's frowning at me, but instead of launching at me to bite my face off, he just nudges my foot like he's asking me to pet him. "Your daddy left specific rules not to pet you. Should we break them?" Who am I kidding? I'm already petting him. His fur is so soft I lose myself there between his ears for a little while. "Mean ol' daddy. You needed some lovin', huh? It's okay, I don't have to listen to his rules. I can't even picture his face." Even admitting that in secret to a dog feels yikes as hell, but he isn't judging me. Or maybe he is. He definitely has a very judgmental face. "Speaking of, I gotta head out, buddy. Pretty sure the one thing I can do is get out before your dad turns up. If he wanted to hang out, he would have."

I place a little kiss on his head, already mourning the idea of never seeing Grumpy Pups again, but I search out my

jensen

pants and shoes as he follows me around like a shadow. Now that I'm walking around, I know without a shadow of a doubt that I didn't hook up with anyone last night, and after using the bathroom and stealing some toothpaste, I slip out of the front door without shame.

It's still a walk of shame, but not for my vagina, and somehow that feels like a win.

The stairs lead me down toward the muffled sound of a jukebox, clueing me in that I'm still at the bar. Maybe the owner let me crash at his place? It feels strange, but maybe that's just how he is. The image of a bunch of drunk people in that amazingly perfect bed makes me shudder, and I hope it isn't some regular occurrence. In fact, I refuse to believe it is. He must have just liked me.

The desire to know what he looks like nearly has me peeking through a window, but that shame rolls its way back up my spine and has me pushing on instead, leaving my knight in shining armor and his adorable dog behind.

the night cap

When I get home fifteen minutes later, I stuff my face with the takeout I grabbed, plug my phone in to charge, and take a long, steaming hot shower. I feel like a new woman when I emerge. The ten text messages from my brothers are the only things that bring me back to reality after I'm dressed in some comfy pajamas. All four of them texted me last night: Gio and Adrian just sent a few random memes, Leo wanted to know if I watched the latest episode of our show, and the rest were all from Xander. The problem with Xander, though, is the fact that I seemed to be drunk texting him before my phone died. Yeah, he's going to lose his shit when he hears from me.

> Have you ever had an Adios?

> The drink? An Adios Motherfucker?

> I don't think that's the name. It has a bad word in it.

> Please don't tell me you're drunk.

jensen

You know I'm the older sistr, right?

I'd take that more seriously if you could spell sister right. Where are you?

I'm at home. Go awy.

The next few have me shocked that he hasn't already kicked in my door.

You're not at home. Home doesn't have Adios unless you bought like seven different liquors.

Where are you?

Calliope!

It's fucking Thursday. Do you at least have tomorrow off?

I swear if you ghost me right now...

Fuck! No one else is answering either. I'm coming home.

the night cap

Home? My eyes widen when I remember he's out of town with his best friends. *Shit!* Hastily, I press the call button and hope with all of me I didn't ruin his vacation. He answers on the second ring, instantly jumping into a lecture like he isn't the baby of the family. "Xan, I'm sorry. I got drunk."

"No shit." He's definitely still mad.

"Yeah. Please tell me you didn't leave your trip?"

Xander sighs. "I didn't because Adrian finally answered and went to make sure you got home okay. He said your living room light was on and that you probably just went to sleep. Did he come inside?"

If he did, he's covering for me. My light was on when I got home and normally I shut all those off, so maybe he did just assume I made it back safely. "No clue. But don't worry about me, okay? I'm not going anywhere today and I won't ever drink again."

"You say that every time. Seriously, Cals. You can't freak me out like that."

His tone changes so suddenly I hear my little brother again, the one scared to lose anyone else. "I promise I won't, okay? I'm fine. Didn't even get laid."

"Gross. Don't." He finally cracks a laugh. "How's your head?"

"Feels like that one time I fell out of the tree. I need to take something."

"Oh, so you haven't taken anything for that?" The asshole yells that so loudly, it rings in my skull and I get the urge to kick him in the nuts.

"You dick. Ugh. Bye! Enjoy your stupid vacation."

He's still laughing, but at least I'm not on his shit list anymore as we hang up and I call Adrian to see if he actually came by. He admits to driving past and not seeing my car in my parking spot, but he figured I was fine because of the light. For once, I'm actually okay with him wanting to rush back to live in his own little world. Sometimes dealing with Adrian is hard. He's one of those guys that is too self-centered to see anything from someone else's point of view, and him being too tired to check in on me fully kept Xander where he is.

It worked out this time.

the night cap

If I'm ever kidnapped, though, I do hope they call literally any *other* brother.

When I get some medicine in my system, I decide to call it a day and head to bed. I have a hangover to sleep off and the earlier shift at work tomorrow, so I send off a couple of return memes to the other brothers and take my ass to bed. I'm coming up on thirty fast and going to bars alone is going to stop being cute soon, but as I drift off, I convince myself to do it a few more times. I'll stop when I get over that thirty mark, but for now… I'm going to enjoy the last dregs of my twenties and I have a strong feeling I want to have this fun at that new bar.

I have an owner to properly meet.

Chapter Two:
The Rerun

Callie

Am I seriously going to do this again?

I stare up at Harvey's Bar with my bottom lip pinched tightly between my teeth.

Yes, yes, I am.

I went with some teal leggings tonight, so I hopefully don't feel inclined to call them bitches and take them off, but I can't make any promises. 'Pants are for bitches' is pretty much my life motto, and my best friend, Reagan — or rather ex-best friend — would have laughed her ass off at that note's accuracy.

Thinking about her makes me miss her. We haven't been talking much in the last few months because she made out with Adrian before he got with his current girlfriend, knowing full well I told her my brothers were off limits. I know that's cliché, but with the older two being married, the only brothers I have to worry about that happening with are the two younger ones — and neither of them is in any sort of position to marry her.

The last thing I need is awkward birthday parties because they had a fling and broke up.

I'll forgive her, especially since they both promised it didn't go past a drunken kiss… I just need a little time.

Walking inside the bar gives me a sense of weird déjà vu, and I silently curse myself for getting so drunk last week that my whole night here is fuzzy. The jukebox next to the dance floor and pool tables is familiar, but the bar isn't and the pristine oak bar top looks handmade. I definitely would have remembered something that nice, wouldn't I?

"Hey, can I get Dirty Shirley?"

No Adios Motherfuckers tonight. That name is way too fitting.

jensen

The bartender smirks when she sees me like we share a secret, tossing her belly button-length purple hair over her shoulder. The commitment that must take is astounding, and I'm even more surprised I don't remember her. "Taking it easy this time?" she asks, pulling a glass on top of the bar to mix my drink. "You went hard last week."

"Yikes, you remember me?" I chuckle. "Yes, taking it much easier tonight… hopefully. I have a knight in shining armor to thank, but not until I get some liquid courage. I can't imagine the shit I did by the time the bar was closing. Tell me now though, should I be running away and never coming back? How bad was I?"

She slides my drink over and leans forward, sizing me up. "You were a mess, sweet girl. And yeah, we all remember you. I'm Daria. The guy behind me is Stephen." Jerking her head toward a tall guy with huge dimples and messy hair, she yells, "Steve! You remember her?"

His eyes drop to me, making me blush — but there's no mistaking the grimace on his face. "Sure do. Feeling better tonight?"

"Yes. Sorry. I feel like I need to say sorry to everyone here," I groan. "Were you the one who made sure I had somewhere to sleep? I swear I don't normally get that fucked up. It was an off day for me."

Stephen shakes his head, suddenly a lot more amused than he'd been two seconds ago. "Nope, that was the boss, Harvey. We tried to get you into a cab, but you kept lecturing us on stranger danger, and your phone was dead so we couldn't call anyone you knew. Harvey took you up to his place."

I take a long drink and glance around for another worker, immediately coming up short. "Well… stranger danger is real, Sir. I guess you were all strangers too, but I must have felt safe here. Where is this boss man? I probably owe him an even bigger apology… especially for the pants thing." My eyes bug out of their sockets as a horrifying thought occurs. "Please tell me that didn't happen down here."

Daria laughs, shaking her head. "I'm not sure what you're talking about, so my guess is no. Harvey's in the back. Do you want me to go get him?"

"Um… maybe after this drink?" I offer sheepishly. "Or two, but I promise not to be a menace tonight."

Humming, she moves on to take care of another customer, but Stephen yells for Harvey as loud as he can before I can take a single sip.

Dick! Stephen is officially on my shit list.

A moment later, a man at least a foot taller than me with rippling, tattoo-covered muscles, a perfectly groomed beard, and eyes so light I can't tell what color they're even supposed to be walks out and snaps, "What?" as he looks around.

The moment he spots me, his entire intimidating frame goes rigid.

Well, shit.

I lean in to sip my drink with a guilty expression, my gaze staying locked with his even though all I want to do is hide. "Hello, Harvey. You look even grumpier than your dog."

Great start, Calliope. Do you ever shut up?

the night cap

"I take that as a compliment. Did you forget something last week?" he asks, voice nearly as rough as it had been when he yelled at Stephen.

Besides my dignity? No.

It makes me feel very unwanted, but I refuse to cower. I'm a paying customer. "Yeah, this drink here. Thanks for the help, by the way."

For a moment, it looks like he's going to laugh — but he doesn't. Instead, he walks closer until I can smell that leather-whiskey-man scent that fills his apartment. "You're welcome. Thank you for not assuming the worst of me."

"No worries. I stand by what I said: pants are for bitches, but my hoo-ha never lies and she would have told me if something happened."

I can hear Stephen laughing from somewhere, but I don't avert my gaze from the giant that smells good or the stunned look on his gorgeous face. "I'm sorry, your what?"

Suddenly, I don't feel so confident about my word choice. "M-My hoo-ha. You know…" I trail off and point down

jensen

under the bar top. "You've dealt with one of those before, right?"

Stephen knocks over an empty beer bottle. "Oh, no she didn't. Daria, run," he hisses, but Harvey doesn't seem fazed.

He shrugs a shoulder and leans against the bar. "Nope. I've dealt with pussies, vaginas, cocks and cunts, but never a hoo-ha. Did you two ID her?"

"Yes," Daria says quickly. "She's twenty-nine."

My gaze narrows. "I was trying not to be crass, *Harv*. But fine, my pussy wasn't fucked and I imagine a big guy like you would have left some aching behind. What do I know, though? The 'big hands' thing is probably a myth."

Don't look at his hands. Don't. Look. At. His. Hands. Oh shit, they're gorgeous.

"My name is Harvey," he rumbles. "But you're right. It's a myth."

Shame. "Good to know. Sorry about that," I mumble, drinking a little more. "Where's Grumpy Pups? Does he ever come down and play?"

"No. Dammit doesn't like people."

"Dammit?" I ask with a laugh. "Did you name your dog Dammit?"

21

the night cap

He grunts. "Yes. If you spend over five minutes with him, you'll understand. Akita's have very... unique personalities."

"Mmhm," I agree, not wanting him to ask if I pet him. Because I absolutely did, and I have no regrets. He seemed to like me just fine. "Is that why you picked him? Like father like son?"

Daria coughs loudly and swipes her hand across her neck, but it's too late. Harvey's already shutting down. He leans forward, slipping a napkin under my drink. "Be safe tonight, Calliope."

No one moves or says a word until he's gone. Daria inches closer, filling my drink up again. "It's a sore spot for him. He was married once. His ex-wife showed up one night with a puppy, then served him divorce papers a week later. The only thing he got when her lawyers were through was the puppy."

"Fuck me," I sigh. "Of course I found the sore spot. I'm great at that. He hates me, doesn't he?"

She reaches over to squeeze my hand. "No. He's grumpy — borderline a dick sometimes — but he doesn't hate you. We have the cops on speed dial around

jensen

here; normally when someone gets too drunk to drive and won't get in a cab, they sleep it off at the station. He wouldn't hear of it with you. Insisted he could put you up for the night."

I frown at my now empty drink and absentmindedly ask for another as I think about that. I mostly want to know why the hell he didn't want me getting tossed in a cell. I can't imagine I was easy to deal with, but I don't ask her. She probably wouldn't know why, anyway. "So, has he ever let anyone stay up there before? Or am I the first?"

"You're the first, but he'll deny it if you ask him. God forbid a man ever show a little softness, huh?"

"I guess so." My phone rings a second later and I sigh when I see Xander's photo on the screen. "Nope, not answering this one. Can I have a shot? Vodka is fine so I'm not mixing."

Chuckling, she lines up two of them and holds one up for herself. "Cheers, girl."

It lifts my mood instantly. I forgot how much fun it is having drinks with a friend. "Cheers. Your hair is gorgeous, by the way. Did I say that last time?"

"Yes." Winking, she backs up to fill someone else's drink, and my attention is pulled to Harvey's office. He's standing there half shrouded in shadow, leaning against the doorframe — and staring directly at me.

He is ridiculously hot. The shadows only make him seem more mysterious than he already is, but the last thing I need is to become enthralled with this grumpy, emotionally unavailable man.

I break our stare when my phone rings again and then take the time to convince my brother I'm on the way home safe. I'm not, though, because for reasons I don't understand, I'm not done with Harvey or his gorgeous bar, so I make my way over to the jukebox and order myself another drink.

No one is here to stop me, anyway.

Oh shit, I did it again.

The smell of his studio surrounds me like a comforting hug, making me once again want to stay there in its warmth, but I seriously need to get the hell out of here.

AND HERE WE ARE AGAIN.
YOU KNOW WHERE YOUR KEYS ARE.
THERE ARE DONUTS ON THE TABLE AND ASPIRIN IN THE MEDICINE CABINET.
SERIOUSLY, THOUGH. STOP PET-TING THE DOG.

I groan. How the hell did he know I pet Dammit last time? The culprit is in the same position he was before, and when I get out of bed, he rubs against me, wanting to be pet. I'm not strong enough to deny a dog love. What kinda monster is? After about five minutes of snuggles on the floor, I make my way into his bathroom to clean up, taking in my disheveled black hair and my exhausted hazel eyes with a frown. I'm a fucking mess, but Harvey keeps me safe instead of sending me to the drunk tank, so it's kind of hard to imagine why I'd stop.

I like the feel up here, and the adorable dog helps too. There are definitely worse places to wake up, and this time, there are donuts next to my keys. Can I really complain?

Harvey might, but I can't.

I take some medicine and down three donuts before I sneak out of his place again. I should probably stay away… but as I glance at the bar in my review mirror, I know I probably won't.

I've never made the best decisions.

Chapter Three: The Proof

Harvey

The urge to go back upstairs and see her is strong enough that the styrofoam coffee cup in my hand is cracking. I ignore the pointed look on Daria's face as I shove the schedule toward her for her approval, because I don't need her shit right now.

Or ever, but that's never stopped her before.

"I'll handle Thursday with you. You and Stephen will take Friday, and I'll be here with him Saturday," I recite, earning me a bitchface.

"If you're going to read me the schedule, why did I have to come in at the ass-crack of dawn? This could've been a phone call. Or a text message. Or an e-mail."

She's right, but I need her here to make sure I stay in my office until Calliope leaves. I can't go up there. "Plausible deniability," I deflect. "Now you can't complain."

"I don't believe you," she argues. "You're avoiding her. Where did you sleep, anyway?"

Sighing, I sit back and toss the pen on my desk. "On the couch again, for the whole two hours I actually slept. I was out of there by six," I admit.

"Of course you were," she crosses her arms. "What happens up there? She apologized for taking her pants off yesterday, but she definitely didn't take her pants off down here."

"That doesn't seem like any of your business, does it?" I level. "I didn't touch her, if that's what you're after." Though fuck me sideways and drag me through hell, I wanted to. I still want to. I want to walk up those stairs, tear the fucking stupid green pants off her gorgeous, thick curves and die between her thighs.

jensen

"Either time, just to be clear. I make sure she pees and has some water and then put her to bed."

"Go figure she called you her knight. You know she's petting the dog, right?" Daria smirks, making me roll my eyes.

"I'm aware. If she gets bit, that's her problem. I warned her."

"He won't bite her. He knows you like her." She arches an eyebrow. "I like her too, by the way… so do all the customers."

For fuck's sake. "I never said I like her. I don't date, Daria. You know that." It's the truth. My ex-wife proved to me that all handing over my heart would do was get it stomped on, so fuck that. I do just fine without it. "Are you okay with the schedule or not?"

Disappointment flashes in her eyes, but she doesn't comment again. She knows better. "Yup. Looks good to me, boss. Want me to text Stephen about it or will you call him in for a special meeting too?"

"Don't be like that. Stephen doesn't care what hours he works, so I was giving you the choice."

the night cap

"Got it. Anything else?" She tosses her hair over her shoulder. "Want me to go up and see if the coast is clear?"

No, because I don't want to know if it's not. "It's alright. I have some errands to run, so no time like the present."

"Alrighty. But for the record, not all of us are dicks like your ex, especially the ones that use words like hoo-ha."

She leaves my office with a chuckle, taking away the only thing stopping me from going back upstairs.

Truthfully, I got over what my ex did to me a long time ago. I go months, even years without giving her a second thought until someone asks me questions about where I got that dog from. It's not Dammit's fault his mom was impossible to please, but still. The reminder of why I've got my walls up so high always puts me in a bad mood.

And Calliope Marino is exactly the type of girl to make it worse, because I can already see exactly how easy it would be to fall for her. The dorky pants, lop-sided smile, the blush that floods her rounded cheeks, the seriously generous curves that have been plastered in my

mind since I first saw her dancing to Brit-
ney fucking Spears… she's everything my
ex wasn't and everything I've always
craved.

Soft, warm, sweet.

It's just not a good idea.

Four hours later, I climb the stairs to
my apartment and pray to god she's gone
and beg the devil to have her sitting on
my couch. The conflicting desires aren't
lost on me, but when I open the door to
find Dammit languishing on the living
room floor and nothing but empty space
around him, I realize I was rooting for
the devil.

He let me down.

Disappointed for reasons I don't want
to think about, I do a once-over of the
apartment to make sure nothing's missing. Not that I think she'd steal from me,
but it never hurts to check — and if I
stop at my bed to smell my pillow, that's
my business. I don't have the range to
know what the hell the scent of her
shampoo is, but I know it's intoxicating,
and I know I'm fucking pathetic for it.

the night cap

Desperate to get my shit together, I head back toward the door and grab Dammit's leash to take him for a walk.

"C'mon, boy," I whistle. The fucker doesn't move, just huffs like a judgmental little asshole and flicks his tail at me. "Get over here, Dammit. Let's go. Time for a walk."

Slowly, he lifts his head and whines, then flops right back down, rolling onto his back to expose his stomach. Proof positive that Calliope was generous with the belly rubs, but now that means I have to do it. Dropping down, I rub his chest and grab his snout playfully. "She's not here. Get over it."

He barks, flipping onto his feet and sitting defiantly.

"She went home, boy. Don't go getting attached, okay? This was a two-time thing." Great, I'm rationalizing with a canine now. "Let's go."

Dammit's eyes narrow to the point where I have to wonder if he understands me, but he finally lets me put the leash on him and lead him out the door.

jensen

He won't go near Daria or Stephen when they come up, so the fact that he took to her so quickly only makes me more determined to stay away from her.

We've been abandoned enough already.

Chapter Four: The Dance

Callie

Yes, I came back again, and no, I don't regret it. Stephen and Daria are fun as hell, and with my shortage of friends and abundance of brothers, this bar is becoming somewhat of a haven for me.

Especially since I know I'm actually safe here.

Four daiquiris in, I'm dancing near the jukebox as tall, broody and mysterious watches from his door frame again, and I can't help but notice how his eyes hardly ever leave me.

Good… I don't want them to.

Needing a break from the fast stuff, I move over to toss on "These Arms of

the night cap

Mine" by Otis Redding then walk up to the big burly door statue and tug on his rough hand. "You're up, boss man. I need a partner for this one."

"Absolutely not," he argues, immovable as he shakes his head. "I don't dance, Calliope."

"And I don't drink," I lie back. "Everyone dances, Harvey. I don't care what you say. You're dancing with me. Put it on my tab."

I tug again, pleased when he stumbles forward a little and lets me drag him out to the middle of the floor.

"This is ridiculous," he argues, but as I spin to face him, his hands find my hips to pull me closer. "You're ridiculous."

"You're ridiculously tall. Are those steel-toe boots necessary?"

"Are your bright pink pants necessary?" he quips.

"Yes, they are, actually. Pretty sure I'm the brightest thing in here and now everyone will notice you're dancing."

He shakes his head with the closest thing to a smile that I've seen yet, but he doesn't stop. He takes my hand, twirling me around in a circle and guiding me in until our bodies are pressed together and the low hum of the song pulses through us, and I have to wonder how long *his* arms have been lonely as Otis sings about it. "I'd be highly surprised if you weren't the brightest thing in every room you've ever been in," he whispers, and the urge to climb him and kiss those grouchy lips overtakes everything. Yeah, I definitely want to fuck him.

"You might not be wrong."

Even to my ears, I sound breathless, but the song ends too soon and Harvey's pulling back. "You got your dance, sunshine."

"One more?" I ask, my bottom lip poking out for good measure, but I seem to have gotten another gentleman's attention by accident.

"If he's done, I'll dance with you, beautiful."

The guy is obviously drunk, and I've had enough shitty experiences with drunk guys to know I don't want him anywhere near me — but the second the smile fades from my face, Harvey is standing between us.

the night cap

"You heard her. She wants another dance with me. Run along," he mutters.

The guy stumbles a little with his hands up. "Didn't know you had claim, big man. Proceed."

"Claim? What am I, a prized pig?"

The man laughs. "Hey, you said it, not me."

I hear the gurgle before my brain actually registers the fact that Harvey punched the guy in the throat. He doubles over, sputtering and cussing, and the whole bar goes silent around us.

"Sorry, what the fuck did you just say to her?" Harvey snaps. "C'mon. On your feet, say that shit to my face. You'd look better without your teeth, anyway."

Daria is by my side in a second, my hands trembling a little as the guy tries to breathe and gasps, "Fuck you!"

"Harvey, it's okay."

He ignores me completely, grabbing Douche by the neck of his shirt and hauling him back up. "The fuck is wrong with you shitstains thinking it's fine to insult a beautiful woman just because she's got the good sense not to want you mouth-breathing all over her? Get out of my bar."

Douche flails, taking a swing at Harvey that falls flat, and I barely have time to gasp before Harv has him by the hair and is dragging him outside.

Jesus, that's hot. He's hot, and now my desire to thank him with more than words has grown. No one has ever done anything like that for me before.

Sure, I have my brothers. They've all punched at least one guy for me in our lives, but this is different, and whether he admits it or not, Harvey definitely called me beautiful.

When he comes back without a scratch, I move over and launch myself into his arms for a hug, melting against his muscular chest as he stands there like a wooden plank.

It takes a few seconds, but slowly, he hugs me back. "We adding that to your tab too, sunshine?"

"Yes," I whisper, feeling a little too vulnerable to be in the middle of a bar. "Thank you. Seriously, you didn't have to. I know I'm... a lot, so thank you."

the night cap

He shakes his head, pulling back to cup my chin and make me look at him. "Listen to me, Calliope. It doesn't matter how a lot or a little you think you are, men like that don't deserve to breathe the same air as you." He seems to realize what he said, clearing his throat. "I'd have done the same for anyone."

Yeah, right. Judging by the still-dumbfounded looks on Daria and Stephen's faces, they've never seen Harvey like this.

I decide to play along anyway, even if my eyes are probably shaped like hearts. "Well, now I feel less special." I stick my tongue out at him and pull away so he can't see my cheesy ass smile. "Shot time!"

Daria snaps into action, pouring a line of them just in time for Harvey to steal one and make his way to his office. "I don't know what spell you put on him," she whispers, "but keep doing it."

I take it easy after that, drinking mostly water and only having one more drink. Pushing my luck seems like a bad idea when I've made so much progress tonight, so I spend the next hour grilling

jensen

Daria about her life whenever she has a moment for me.

Closing time comes a little too fast.

Every time the lights click on in a bar, I feel like a vampire being exposed to the sun, but when my giant knight walks out of his office, I smile at how grumpy he looks even without the shadows surrounding him. "I know I know. It's time to go."

"No. Give me your keys," he says, holding out his hand.

There's no world where I can drive right now, but something about being asked for my keys makes me want to say no. I'd do anything to give my grump a hard time. "What keys?"

I cross my arms and stand taller, laughing when it makes no difference next to him and only makes him pinch his brows.

"Calliope."

The growl in his voice sends a shiver down my spine, making me bite my lip as I pull them out and plop them into his delicious hand. "So grouchy. Are you finally going to have me tossed in the drunk tank?"

the night cap

"Should I?"

I'm sure my smug expression falters a little. "No. I can get an Oob. No need to call the po-po."

Those unnaturally light eyes close for the briefest of moments. "I'm going to pretend you didn't say that. But fine, if you'd rather call an Uber, be my guest. As long as you're not driving."

"Fine." I go to pull my phone out only to find it missing from my back pocket, but Daria appears with it and hands it over. "Thank you. You're a lifesaver. There isn't a purple flavored Lifesavers candy, is there? There should be."

"One of the gummies is purple," Dalia offers. "Harvey, are you sure it's a good idea that she takes an Uber home?"

"It's her choice," he says quietly. "And hers alone."

"I'll be fine. If the wait is long, I'll just call Xander. It's whatever."

I pull open the app and start walking toward the door, nearly running smack into it. Harvey grabs my shoulders and pulls me back at the last second, then sighs like he's angry with himself. "Cal-

liope, either call your brother or get upstairs. Uber is no longer an option."

"I thought it was my choice," I argue,
but as soon as I see a car is thirty minutes
away, I sigh. "Fine. I'll call Xan… how'd
you know that was my brother's name?"

"The first night you stayed with me,
you rambled about how he was going to
murder you for letting your phone die. It
was right before you insulted pants and
nearly cracked your skull falling over." He
backpedals, nodding to Daria with a tight
jaw and disappointment in his eyes.
"Make sure she gets in his car safely."

Spinning on his heels, he walks back
toward his office as Daria swats my arm
and hisses, "You idiot! He invited you
this time and you'd rather go with your
brother?"

"Invited me where?" I ask, confused,
then the options he offered get clearer.
"Oh, he said go upstairs? I thought… we
were talking about an Uber and I thought
he just wanted me gone."

I glance at where he left and hesitate,
but she pushes me forward. "No, he invited you upstairs. He fought a man for
you tonight. Go tell him your brother

didn't answer and pout your lip again. Go."

"Okay," I whisper back sharply, then walk over to his office. "He didn't answer, so I'm taking you up on your generous offer to go upstairs. Thank you, knight."

Harvey keeps his head down, scribbling numbers on a paper. "Have Daria walk you up there. You know where everything is."

I don't say anything at all as I turn around and fake a smile at Daria. "He's mad at me. I didn't even realize he offered that, but I guess I can't blame the booze for everything. It's fine, I'll get out of his hair as soon as possible. He said for you to walk me up if that's cool?"

She sighs. "You two are hopeless, but yeah. Come on."

I follow her up the stairs and immediately drop down to greet Dammit. "Hey, boy. I've missed you. At least you're not mad at me, huh?"

He licks my face, then growls at Daria, chasing her back out onto the landing of the steps. "Whoa, boy. Just delivering her for you."

jensen

"Hey," I chastise. "That wasn't nice. Daria is a good friend… you like friends, don't you?" I turn to her. "Does he do that a lot?"

"To literally everyone who isn't Harvey. Harvey talks a big game about hating this dog, but they're inseparable. He'd take a bullet for him, and I'm pretty sure Dammit knows it. Won't go to anyone but him and apparently you."

Dammit sits, looking up at me with his signature bitchface, so I kiss his head to show them both I don't fear him. "Well, now I feel special again. Thanks, Daria. I'll probably see you soon."

She smiles, hesitating for only a moment, then pauses in the doorway. "Look, I like you. You're sweet and fun… and I don't want to see you get hurt. Be careful here, okay? Harvey's got walls taller than he is. Have a good night."

Tapping the doorframe, she heads out and leaves me alone — but not for long.

Before I can even slip out of my pants and hide my legs under his comforter, the door opens and he gets a clear view of my ass. "Shit. Sorry I — pants are for bitches, remember?"

the night cap

His eyes darken. "I think I'm finally starting to believe you about that." Bending down, he scratches behind Dammit's ears. "Do you need anything?"

"I need to pee. Sorry for being a brat earlier, by the way. I really wanted to see our dog."

"Our?" He squints at me as I shimmy back out of bed, padding past him toward his bathroom.

"Yes, ours. Dammy loves me. I even got kisses today."

The poor man doesn't breathe for a solid ten seconds. "So you're disobedient *and* a brat, hm?"

Why the fuck did that just make me wet? Holy hell.

I rush to pee and steal some toothpaste, squirming slightly before I leave the safety of the bathroom. "I don't think I'm a brat. I just do bratty things sometimes."

"And pet dogs you're asked not to," he adds, handing me a bottle of water. "Drink this."

"Yes, sir." I do an embarrassing salute and poke my eye, cursing slightly as I take a small sip. "How did you expect me

46

not to pet him? Look at him. He's such a little babe. I love dogs. I'm a dog aunt, y'know?"

Harvey grunts. "Most people have enough self-preservation instincts to avoid dogs they're told not to pet, but you don't seem to have any self-preservation at all."

"Hey, that's mean. I just feel safe here, and he was nice to me. He never even growled at me."

"Doesn't sound like Dammit, but I don't see any bite marks so I'll have to take your word for it." His eyes drop slowly, lingering on my exposed thighs. "Sure you'll be warm enough?"

"You have a warm bed." I spin around to go climb inside and I can feel his eyes on my ass. It makes me have to bite back a smile. "Or you can come keep me warm."

He's silent for so long, I'm not sure if he heard me — but when I peek my head up to see him, he's still standing there. "You've had too much to drink, Calliope. Get some sleep."

The light flicks off a moment later, and I watch him move around in the dark, wishing I could figure out a way to convince him. "Night, Harvey. Maybe I'll actually see you in the morning."

"I've got some things to do early. Just lock up whenever you leave."

"You got it." With a sigh, I melt into his bed and stare off into the dark. One day I might have to accept the fact that he may never let me past his tall walls, but by the time I'm drifting off, I know I'm still not ready to give up on him.

Not yet, at least.

Chapter Five: The Rules

Harvey

How am I supposed to sleep with her half naked in my bed?

My cock is so hard in my jeans that I'm seconds away from doing something I'll regret. I know she's not drunk, at least not as drunk as the first two times we did this, but even two drinks would've still been too many.

I refuse to take advantage of her.

Still, the memory of her thick thighs and round ass is plastered in my mind as I listen to her snore quietly. What I wouldn't fucking give to crawl into bed behind her, slide a hand over her gorgeous, exposed stomach and hold her until she forgets every man who ever came before me.

It's clearly been too long since I've gotten laid.

This is dangerous. It's stupid. Everything about her is ridiculous, from her pants to the way she says things. She will *not* be the girl to make me put my heart on the line again. It's just not possible.

And yet… no.

No, no, no.

Nope.

After about twenty minutes of sleep, I wake up with the sun and quietly change my clothes. At some point, Calliope threw the comforter off of her and her stunningly beautiful body is on full display for me, but I don't let my dick make decisions before breakfast. I have a hard rule that I don't get involved with anyone associated with the bar, whether they're employees or customers, and this is no exception.

I need to get out of here.

Without Daria to distract me, though, my errands don't take me nearly as long as I thought. I have the same argument with god and the devil that I did last time, but for once, the devil's the one in charge. When I open the door with two bags of breakfast takeout in my hand, I find Callie looking like she just finished washing up. She still isn't wearing any pants, and to top it off, Dammit is glued to her side like she belongs here. "Morning, Harvey. I must have slept in late."

My stomach squirms. "Oh. Lucky you, then. I brought breakfast."

"Really?" Her eyes drop to the bags and she smiles. "Thanks. Do I need to wear pants?"

Licking my lips, I let my eyes wander down her frame again. I'd sooner set fire to those ludicrous pants than let her put them back on, but this will be easier if she makes the right choice on her own. "That's up to you."

With a shrug, she waltzes over to help me lay everything out, her hips swaying to a tune I can't hear. "I swear you have the best bed in the world."

Keep your shit together, Harvey. This girl is bad news. "Mhm. This isn't a hotel, Miss Marino. Don't get any ideas."

the night cap

"Well, you have to pay for hotels…" she trails off, eyes flicking toward my crotch without shame before going right back to the food.

There's no way her mind just went to the same place mine did, but fuck. Now I can't see anything except her on her knees for me.

"You're racking up quite a tab, Calliope."

"I am, aren't I?"

The second she sucks her finger into her mouth to hide a smirk, I sit down to hide something very different under the table.

Fuck me, she looks good with her cheeks hollowed out. "Eat your breakfast."

"Bossy bossy," she teases, sitting right next to me before she listens. "So, how does your giant-self sneak out so silently every morning?"

"Easy. I wait until you start snoring." I take a bite of my bagel and do my best to stifle a laugh as she gapes at me.

"I do not! You do!"

She blushes so enticingly that it's hard to imagine going a day without seeing it, but the suddenness of that thought has me balking a little.

"You do snore," I deadpan. "I'll record it for you next time."

"Don't." Her foot flies out to kick my shin softly. "Don't ruin the fantasy that I look like a princess while sleeping. I will cry."

"Calliope," I scold gently. "Why? Princesses are… fake. They're cookie-cutter, too perfect, and boring. You are none of those things, and that's something to be proud of."

She smiles at me, those hazel eyes locked with mine as she accepts my answer with a small nod. "Be careful, Harvey. It almost sounds like you don't mind having me around."

Fuck.

I wish I could tell her how strange this is. That I haven't let a woman stay overnight since my ex left. That other than Daria, I've never let another woman inside this apartment. That having her here, pantsless, blushing and eating breakfast with me like it's the most normal thing in the world is simultaneously comforting and painful as hell.

the night cap

I don't want this to be normal; I don't want her here; I don't want to fall in love.

Yet as she sneaks a piece of bacon to Dammit and scratches behind his ears with something a lot like love in her eyes, I'm not sure she's going to give me a choice.

Breakfast ends all too soon, the dishes disappearing into the sink before I can tell her to leave them, but when she walks back toward me, she doesn't stop until she's sinking down on her knees and glancing up at me. "Let me pay you back for everything, big guy."

Her small hands reach out for my jeans, and for a moment, I can't do anything but stare at her. I want it so badly, I can taste it, but I have rules. Lines. And one of them is not letting people pay me with sex, and that's what this is. "Calliope," I groan out, forcing myself to take a step back and gently grab her hands. "You don't need to repay me like that. I — no."

jensen

She stays where she is, hands dropping to her thighs while that blush deepens. "I know I don't need to. I want to."

Fuck. Why? What the hell did I do to the universe that led to me being tortured like this? My vision is blurry I want her so badly, but rules. Lines. "Not like this," I whisper, guiding her back to her feet. "I think we should talk."

She moves away from me once she's standing and grabs her pants, slipping them on before she waves a hand at me to speak. "Okay."

It's hard not to see the walls she's putting up, not when I'm so intimately familiar with my own. "I don't date as a general rule, but I definitely don't get involved with customers or employees of the bar. You're — hell, Calliope. You're beautiful."

"Thank you, and understood. I'll find a better way to thank you." She slips on her shoes and drops down to say goodbye to Dammit before closing the distance between us to kiss my cheek. "See you next week, Harv."

the night cap

The nickname normally grates on my nerves, but here, I know I have bigger problems. She's about to walk out the door… I just can't seem to make words come out of my stupid mouth in an order that'll make her understand.

Maybe I don't understand, either.

"Next weekend," I agree, slipping my hands into my pockets. "Drive safe."

Chapter Six: The Payment

Callie

Although the denial hurt my pride a little, I know better than to take it personally.

It wasn't because of the usual reasons I've been denied. I believe him when he tells me I'm beautiful, and I don't think he's the type of guy to shy away from a thicker woman. Those insecurities will always live under the surface, but I don't think they're a factor here. Beauty and attraction aren't enough for him. Those trust issues run deep, and some drunk girl showing up for three weeks isn't going to change that. I don't know what happened with his ex, and frankly, it isn't my business, so as I walk inside Harvey's and move straight over to the bar, I tell myself I won't drink at all.

I have a plan. I'll help around the bar as a thank you, have sober conversations with him if he'll let me, then go on my way so I'm not a burden.

Plans never go wrong, right?

"Hey, Daria. I'm not here for fun. Just tell me how I can help around the bar."

"Did Harvey send you?" she asks, cocking her head to the side. "I didn't know we were hiring anyone else."

"You're not. This is just me thanking him and all of you guys for everything. I'm even wearing practical pants."

They're black leggings, but my shirt is bright yellow for all the times he called me sunshine. I couldn't walk out of the house without a bit of color.

"Does he even know you're here?"

"No," I admit. "Are you going to tell on me?"

I pout my lip as amusement lines her face and she hands me a rag. "Oh, this oughta be good. He's in the back, so I don't have to tell on you at all. He'll see for himself soon enough. He's bartending with me tonight."

"Oh." For some reason, that makes me laugh. "Should be fun then."

I have to go on my toes to wipe off the bar top, but the tables and booths prove to be easy. There are plenty of water marks and beer stains to keep me busy, and by the time I move back toward the bar, there's more to clean there, too.

With work like this, time is going to fly by and I already enjoy this more than my actual job.

When the rush starts, Harvey comes out from the back and starts mixing drinks, not noticing me. Daria keeps looking between us like she's waiting to see Santa Claus pop up or something, and her excitement for this is contagious. I want to see his reaction almost as much as she does.

When the suspense starts to make me anxious, I move behind the bar to clean off my rag and bump him with my hip as I squeeze by. "'Scuse me, boss."

Grunting, Harvey tenses as looks around like he's being Punk'd. "You don't work here."

the night cap

"Tonight I do." I shrug and move on, smiling to myself as I imagine the shock on his face.

"I think she's doing pretty good, Harvey."

I can hear the amusement in Daria's voice as Harvey mutters something I can't quite make out, but then he's behind me and gripping the bar top with both hands to cage me in. I don't know what's hotter, the action, the tattoos I see snaking down his arms to his fingers, or the way his breath feels against my ear. "I'm not paying you, Calliope. I don't need another employee."

"I didn't ask you to pay me," I whisper, but I know he can hear me. I couldn't make my voice louder if I tried. It's been far too long since a man has made me feel this way. "I told you I'd find a better way to thank you."

He hums, deep and promising, then steps back to grab a beer from the cooler. "So this is how you're choosing to work off that tab of yours?"

"Mmhmm, my first offer was denied. Do you have a better idea?"

jensen

I meet his gaze and stand tall, not that it helps much. "May—" the phone rings, making both Harvey and Daria look at it like they've never seen it before. It's a landline hanging next to the mirror that stretches almost all the way along the back wall, and for all the times I've been here, I've never heard it ring once. "That thing is still active?" he asks, taking the few steps to answer it. "Hello?" His eyes narrow. "No, you don't." Pause. "That's exactly what I'm saying. Try again."

I meet Daria's eyes to see if she has a clue who would be calling and she shrugs. "Do only employees have that number?"

"I don't even have it," she hisses as the look on Harvey's face gets angrier.

"Goddamnit, boy. You couldn't have picked a worse time for this. Good luck."

The receiver slams back down and no one moves for a moment.

"Telemarketer?" Daria offers.

"No. Stephen doesn't work here anymore. I'll need you here the next two nights with me."

My eyes widen as worry for Stephen bubbles to the surface, but I can't focus on that. Harvey might actually need me. "You wanna hire me now?"

His attention snaps to me. "No, Calliope. I don't want to hire you."

"She has a point," Daria argues. "I can't be here tomorrow. So you can either hire her or be on your own, boss. I'm sorry."

Harvey's face tightens. "She hasn't even interviewed."

"Fine. Let's go interview."

I toss the rag aside and stroll on back to his office, not waiting to see if he's going to follow me.

Seeing it for the first time, I notice it looks a lot like his house — organized and plain, with mostly neutral colors and an extremely old jukebox in the corner.

I'm just about to check it out when I hear the door close behind me. "Are you sure about this?" he asks, skirting around me to take a seat at his desk.

"Yes," I rush out, moving to sit in a chair across from him. "Why wouldn't I be?"

He looks speechless for a moment, those eyes of his looking greyer than anything in the harsh lightning. "I don't know. Do you have any experience at all as a bartender?"

"Not a bartender, but I know how to drink," I joke, but it falls flat. "Kidding. I work at Wrapz Burritos, so I have plenty of experience with customer service and your regulars already love me so I know they'd be nice while I learned the ropes."

He studies me for a long moment. "Why do you want this job, Calliope?"

"Because I'm sick of wrapping burritos for a living. I mean, I've been there so long I don't actually have to wrap anymore, but still. I want a change. I like everyone here, and the energy of your bar is addictive."

Plus, you won't touch me either way, so I may as well get paid to look at you so I feel a little less alone when I crawl in my bed at night.

God, that's pathetic.

Something changes with his body language. His shoulders curl in, his lips dip down, and his voice drops. "Fine. Any criminal history I should know about?"

"Yeah, I robbed a bank last week." I laugh. "Of course not. I'm a good girl."

He grunts. "Are you?"

the night cap

"Most of the time," I admit, then stand so we can get back to work. "I'm far from perfect, remember? Also, do you want me to bring you my resume?"

"I wasn't done with you, Calliope." Yet he gets to his feet anyway, tugging the bottom of his fitted black tee down. "Yes. Bring me your resume. You can hold off on the rest of it, though. You've got sixty days to prove to me you won't over pour and that you can hold your own. We'll discuss more permanent arrangements at that point. You'll be paid under the table until then."

My smile grows and I move around to hug him. "Thanks! It's going to be so fun!"

He hugs me a little easier this time, holding me longer than most would. "You and I have very different definitions of the word fun, Calliope. Don't touch the music."

"What?" I pull back, then decide to take that as a joke because there's no way he actually means that. "You're funny. Let's get out there, handsome. Daria needs us."

Chapter Seven: The Trial Run

Harvey

What the hell did I just do?

I watch her walk back out to the floor with my jaw slack. There's no way I just hired her, even temporarily. And two months? Did I have a fucking aneurysm?

Clearly.

Cautiously, I follow her out and try to ignore the way she's whispering to Daria. It's just hard when Daria glances over at me with a huge grin and a wink.

Calliope waves at a patron who asks for two fingers of something I can't hear, and when the girl pours it perfectly, I don't know what the hell to do. I can't have her working here, but the way she looked when she mentioned how she wanted to get out of Wrapz had turned me into a fucking puddle. She knows my rules, and she chose this anyway.

Which means I need to forget what she looks like with her panties and blushing cheeks and flirty glances.

She's an employee now.

Fuck me sideways.

"That was good," I offer, trying to psych myself into accepting this. "Almost too good for someone who hasn't studied mixology or tended bar before."

"I studied all week," she admits. "I can't toss bottles around my shoulders or anything, but I can mix a Sex on the Beach like it's the only action I'm getting. Which it is, but we're not going there." She laughs freely and spins around. "Want me to show you?"

The last thing in the world I need right now is her saying the word 'sex' ever again. My eyes are burning, begging to drop and look past that fluorescent fucking yellow shirt to the generous curves of her ass, the little peek of belly I can see, the hips I want to grab onto and pin to my fucking bed as I sink inside her.

jensen

Briefly, I have to wonder if I'll be the one who quits at the end of two months.

"Stick to what customers order," I mutter.

"You got it, Boss."

For the next hour, she does great. I watch her toss together the popular ones: Old Fashioned, Manhattan, even a couple of White Russians, but when someone orders a Rob Roy, she looks like she wants to hide. "Coming right up." She forces a smile and then spins toward me with wide eyes. "Help. What's a Bob Roy?"

"Rob," I correct, stepping up beside her to grab a glass. "One and a half ounces of single malt, an ounce of sweet vermouth, three dashes of bitters… and a cherry." I slide the finished drink to one of my regulars, then tip my head toward her. "This is Callie, if you haven't already met her. Make sure you let me know if she lets you down."

"How could a pretty girl ever let me down?"

He winks at her and turns away, and Calliope has the nerve to stick her tongue out at me. "Thanks, grumpy."

the night cap

"You're welcome, sunshine." I fight the urge to spank her, reminding me forcefully why I can't fuck my coworkers. I have a definite problem keeping my hands to myself. "How did you get here tonight?"

"My car. I don't plan on drinking, so I won't take over your bed tonight. I know that's getting old."

I don't know whether to be relieved or disappointed. This woman has me so mixed up and ass backward it's almost insulting, but I nod all the same and pick up my phone to change the playlist echoing over the main bar speakers. "Good to know."

The way she watches me with her bottom lip between her teeth tells me she's just as confused as I am here, but I don't miss the disappointment in her eyes. She turns to go back to work, clapping a little too excitedly when someone actually orders a Sex on the Beach. "Hell yes. I got you, girl."

I spend too much time watching her and not enough time taking care of my bar, so when Daria calls me out about it and sends me to the back to tap a new keg, I'm not surprised that she follows me. "Don't say it," I warn her. "Just don't."

"Say what?" she asks, but the amused expression hasn't left her face. "You're just watching your new employee like you watch all of us, right?"

"Yes," I lie. "I may not have had to watch you when you started, but this is normal. She's not a bartender."

"Looks like one to me," she sing-songs. "Yeah, she needs a little help, but she's doing better than most do. Remember Stephen on his first day?"

Unfortunately yes, but I want to think about him even less right now. "Looking isn't a crime, Daria. Did you come back here to yell at me for having eyes?"

She shrugs, crossing her arms like she isn't backing down yet. "She has a nice ass, doesn't she?"

Not. Fucking. Fair. "I thought I just admitted I have eyes?" I quip. "She's beautiful. Every inch of her. This isn't a secret."

She smirks, but I watch it fade almost instantly. "No, it's not. Too bad it doesn't change anything, right?"

the night cap

"No, it doesn't. Especially not now that she's employed here."

Daria scoffs, turning to walk away. "Yeah, that's the reason."

I don't stop her from leaving. She's never made it a secret that she thinks I'm an idiot — the amount of "not all women are your ex" lectures I've gotten from her could fill a book, but she doesn't get it. It's not that I want to be alone forever, it's that I'm a fucking coward. Every time I even consider the possibility of letting someone in, I stop being able to breathe. The problem isn't that I'm heartless. It's that I've always cared too much.

Always.

When it's finally time to close, I make sure Daria gets to her car safely, then turn back to Calliope. "You did well tonight," I say honestly. The poor girl is sweating and looks exhausted, but she kept up with our late rush and learned quicker than I would've guessed. "You don't have to stay. I usually clean and lock up by myself. You guys work hard enough as it is."

"I don't mind." She waves a hand, grabbing a broom without asking how she can help. "It was still fun, but also hard as hell. You keep up with people like a champ. How long have you had this bar?"

"Five years this June." I flip the chairs on top of the table I just wiped down, distracting myself enough to get the right words out. "I was a carpenter before this, but when my ex-wife left, I wanted something that couldn't be taken away from me. The former owner wanted to retire and gave it to me for cheap, so I remodeled, rebranded, and moved in upstairs. I can't imagine doing anything else now."

I side-eye her, waiting for some shocked reaction at the fact that I was married once, but she doesn't seem fazed in the slightest. Either she's playing it cool… or Daria already told her.

"Well, I'm glad you found something that makes you happy. I'm sure you were a hot carpenter, but you were made to be boss man." She leans on the broom and

the night cap

eyes me. "You want to talk about her or is that a no-no conversation?"

"Neither of those things?" I chuckle, flipping a couple more chairs. "We were married for a few years and I thought everything was fine. She didn't. She left me, took my house, and that was that. Honestly, I hadn't thought about her much until you asked why I picked Dammit. How many brothers do you have?"

She starts sweeping again, seemingly happy that I opened up. "Four. I'm the middle child, so… growing up was interesting. The older two are married. I have two nieces and two dog nieces. I swear one of them better give me a nephew someday."

The urge to know everything about every single one of them creeps up my spine until the curiosity is seeping out of my mouth. "How old are the kids? What do your brothers do? Do you get along with their spouses?"

Jesus, I haven't asked that many questions in years. For the first time, it's my turn to blush, and I take the opportunity to turn my back on her and gather the trash from near the door.

jensen

It only worsens when she chuckles. "They're five and three. They're at that stage where they want to be independent, but they're too short. It's the cutest. My oldest brother Giovanni's wife is nice. We didn't really get along in the beginning, but that was years ago now and she's less crazy these days. She just didn't like how close we all were and didn't want to share him. Then there's Leo, and his husband is the best. They travel a lot and he sends me more pictures than my brother, but they're absolutely perfect for each other. What was the other question? Oh. Their jobs. Gio's an accountant. Boring, but he likes numbers, and Leo is a kindergarten teacher. The guy loves kids, just doesn't want one of his own. Then there's the younger two. Adrian has a new job every year. At the moment, he's trying to get a job with my younger brother Xander. He does sheet metal stuff, so he commutes about an hour for work sometimes and we all know Adrian is not cut out for that level of work. Sorry, I'm rambling now. There's just so many of them I could probably talk for hours."

the night cap

And I could listen to her talk longer than that. "Do you have a favorite?"

Her chuckle fills the bar. "Am I allowed to pick a favorite? Or is it just parents that shouldn't?"

"Parents have favorites too. They just don't announce them to the kids," I say. "But sometimes they do. My older brother's name is Bruce, for instance, so I'll give you a second to figure out who the favorite is there."

"No way it isn't you," she quips. "I won't hear it. Is it just you two?"

"Mmhm." I pause, wondering if she honestly didn't get it. "You've seen *Batman*, right?"

I see the moment it clicks. "Oh, my god! Harvey Dent? Is that you?"

"If you're asking if I'm two-faced, no. But yes, my parents named my older brother after the hero and me after the villain. I was the child they didn't want, but it's a mostly funny joke now."

"That's so mean," she pouts, closing the distance between us so she can hug me again. "You're no villain… just a little grouchy, but it's part of your charm."

jensen

She's so short the top of her head barely reaches my chest, but my arms somehow fit around her like they've always belonged there. I don't understand any of this; why she's so warm and easy to talk to, why she keeps putting herself in my space even knowing I'm damaged goods.

But what I *do* know… is that it feels really fucking good.

Chapter Eight: The Moment

Callie

The fact that Harvey opened up to me at all feels really nice. I know it isn't something he does with just anyone, so I'm starting to believe that maybe I'm not the only one here that sees the potential for more. Maybe he isn't ready to admit he likes me just yet, but it's a step in the right direction at least, and I'm feeling hopeful. It's not like I'm falling for him or anything, but I like him, and I find myself drawn to him more with each passing day. He isn't just some grouchy, scorned bar owner. There are layers to him… and I'm dying to get him to open up a little more, even if we end up just being friends.

As long as he fucks me at least once, that is. God, I need to know what it's like to be manhandled by someone of his stature. I can't help it.

I see him watching me as he fills up some beers for a group of guys that are already getting rowdy, and that makes me turn toward Daria with a mischievous grin. "So Boss Man and I opened up about our families last night," I say in a teasing tone. "He must be second-guessing this entire trial period these days, huh?"

"What?" She glances at Harvey. "You actually used words? I didn't know you knew how to do that."

"I don't have any idea what she's talking about," he deadpans. "Sounds like she might've hit her head."

I roll my eyes at him and put a hand on my hip. "Really? A head injury? That's what you're going with?"

"Mmhm." Nodding to another customer, he grabs a bottle of beer for them and turns to me with a shrug as he adds it to their tab. "What you're describing doesn't sound like me."

"You make it sound like I said you smiled or something," I argue. "Now *that* would be insanity."

Daria laughs. "I've known the man for ten years and I've only seen him smile twice. You've got a point."

"That's because you're not funny," he points out. "Maybe I'd smile if the two of you would get back to work."

I mock him in my best impression of a manly voice and get back to work, smiling at the customer in front of me. I know my face still looks flirtatious; it isn't something I can just wipe away, but it's obvious the guy thinks it's for him. "Hey, what can I get for you?"

"A double shot of you, maybe." He sticks his tongue out between his teeth like he thinks it's sexy, then nods behind me to the wall of liquor. "But for now, I'll take a double shot of Jamie."

"You got it," I turn with a blush, not sure of how I'm supposed to react here. Most men leave me alone when my giant boss is hovering around, but this one doesn't seem to care.

the night cap

I pour his liquor, sliding it over to him with a forced smile, and he grips my wrist to pin my hand down before I can let go of the glass. "How bout you take one of these with me? We can have a little party of our own when the lights go down."

I didn't even see Harvey move, but I absolutely see him a split second before he slams Blondie's face into the bar top and yanks it back up by his hair, sending blood spraying all over. "Apologize for touching her," Harvey growls. "Or next time I'll break more than your nose."

"What the fuck, man? Are you insane?" the man yells, the bar going deathly quiet around us. "I didn't know she was taken. She was giving me the 'fuck me' eyes!"

"No, I wasn't!" I argue, rubbing my wrist where he grabbed and the reddened skin shows how hard he was holding me. "Asshole."

Harvey's eyes go black when he sees the damage, and for the second time, I watch him drag someone out of the bar.

"Someone should probably go stop him," Daria says, snapping her fingers when she spots Red, one of our regulars.

jensen

"He's gonna kill the guy and I don't want to pay his bail. Help?"

"Shit," he cusses, rushing out after him and I can't stop my feet from following him.

"I don't want him to get arrested."

I make it outside just in time to see Red pulling Harvey back, but it's clear the damage has been done. The bastard's standing there with blood pouring down his face and cradling his left hand, the one he'd grabbed me with.

"F-Fucking psycho," he mumbles, tripping a little in his hurry to run off, and Harvey waves like he might honestly have a screw or two loose.

The moment he spots me, he rushes over to check my wrist. "Do you need ice?"

"No, I'm fine," I rush out, checking his face for any injuries at all and relaxing when I see he's okay. "You didn't have to do that, hero."

The urge to kiss him is so strong I nearly dive right in, but Harvey's staring after the guy. "I'm nobody's hero, Calliope. That's a dumb term."

the night cap

He pushes past me to go inside, and I could feel some type of way about that — but I can't stop the grin from spreading across my face.

I go back inside with Daria, and although our playful mood has been stomped on, I refuse to let it die tonight. "You do that for all your employees then, boss?"

Harvey grabs the bottle of Jack Daniels and drinks straight from it. "Of course I do."

"Excuse me?" Daria cuts in. "Like hell you do."

It confirms exactly what I wanted it to confirm when I said it, and I smile at him like I've won something. "Maybe not that dumb a term then, huh? Would you prefer knight in shining armor?"

I see the wheels turning behind his gorgeous blue eyes as he tries to find a comeback for that and falls short. "He touched you. Anyone would've done the same."

"The last time someone put his hands on me here, you told me to — and I quote — use the weapons at my disposal," she pushes. "Don't try to act like this is equal treatment. You like her."

"You kicked his ass worse than I would've." Harvey scoffs. "You made him cry."

Suddenly, Daria looks quite proud of herself, and even though I'm proud of her too, I cross my arms over my chest. "You don't think I could have done the same?"

"I never said that," he grumbles, grabbing the bottle and spinning on his heels to go back to his office.

Daria's barely concealing a giggle. "He doesn't care if you could do it on your own or not. I'm telling you, he's never been like this with anyone else. I can count on *no* hands the amount of fights he's been in at this bar before you started coming around, and now he's been in two."

It makes me feel kind of guilty, but it also gets me hot in all the right ways. "I'm going to go in there," I say more to myself than anything, then turn toward her. "Cover for me?"

the night cap

The crowd thinned out a lot when Harvey went ballistic, so Daria grins. "I got you, girl. Go get your man."

It should embarrass me that I practically run over there, but it doesn't. Not even when I close the door behind me and stare at the stunned man before me. "I've never been in a fight before," I admit, moving closer before he can respond. "The most I've ever done is slap Adrian after he tripped me and I felt so guilty after, I cried. I could never have done what Daria did… but you made sure I didn't have to. Twice."

"How about we agree now that you won't make me do it a third time?" he asks quietly. "I almost didn't let him walk away."

"I never meant for the other two to happen either, but I promise not to bring attention to myself if that will help. I'll start wearing dark clothes or something, I don't know."

The crashing disappointment on his face surprises me, but not as much as the whispered, "Calliope," that follows. "Don't do that. This wasn't your fault and I'm sorry for even sort of suggesting it."

I don't remember how we got this close, but I don't dare to move. "You have nothing to apologize for, Harvey. You protected me, and I just want to say thank you. Plus, I'm glad you're not actually a knight. You're too hot when you're angry to cover yourself up in some armor."

"I'll never let anyone hurt you, sunshine," he whispers. "Knight or not."

I bite my lip, fingers curling at my sides with the desire to lunge at him and do what I know we're both craving. "I know."

He meets my eyes for a long moment, then shakes his head slowly as he reaches up to brush his thumb over my bottom lip. "What are you doing to me, woman?"

"I don't know… but I'm not going to stop. You're stuck with me now, grumpy."

Rough hands cup my face and tip my head back as desperate, sure lips meet mine. Harvey kisses me like he hates me, like he loves me, like he doesn't care at all that my knees are turning to jelly and my heart forgot to keep beating.

the night cap

It's so much more than I ever imagined it would be. It feels as if I've never been kissed before, like this kiss is exactly what every fairy tale in existence has ever been about, the ones that bring people back from the brink of death. And in a way, it does. I feel him coming to life again as he owns me and I cling to him like I'll never let go.

But he does. Panting and eyes closed, Harvey breaks the kiss and steps back just enough to give me space. His fists curl at his sides. "I'm so sorry. We can't — this can't happen."

"It's okay," I whisper, taking one step toward him for more, but I feel the barrier between us again, and it's as strong as ever. "Okay," I concede. "I'll get back to work."

When he doesn't move to stop me, I turn away and close his door behind me. Our moment is over, yet my heart rate hasn't gotten the memo as I walk back in a daze. And as I get back into a groove serving, I decide that maybe that singular moment might have ended, but ours hasn't. I refuse to accept it's over before it's even begun.

I refuse.

Chapter Nine: The Temptation

Callie

Over the last couple of weeks, Daria and I have gotten close, and Harvey hasn't mentioned the kiss once. Granted, I haven't either, but I'm done playing nice. I only have so much patience. She's here at my house helping me pick an outfit, and although I don't think a skirt is practical, she seems adamant about it. "Really? A corset too? Can I at least wear some black shorts with it instead of a skirt?"

"That depends. Do you want Harvey to keep snubbing you or do you want to have him eating out of the palm of your hand?" she asks, arms crossed and brows raised. "Because I know him, sweet pea. I know all the things that make him tick."

Definitely the second one. I've wanted him this entire time, but ever since we opened up and talked about our families, I haven't been able to get him off my mind. That kiss sure didn't hurt, either. "Okay, I trust you."

"Then go with the skirt. Some guys get stupid about a little bit of curves, a little bit of pouch, but not him. The one and only time I've ever seen him drunk, he rambled for forty-five minutes about how attractive he finds thicker women who have the confidence to show it off. Most of it was just him repeating he's an ass man and likes how warm and soft they are, but he forbid me from telling anyone that. Whoops." She laughs, picking up the skirt and handing it to me. "Put it on."

How much I enjoyed hearing that is embarrassing, but I take the skirt and let her help me dress, finishing the outfit with some boots that gave me a couple of inches. "I might actually reach his chin tonight."

jensen

"Screw the chin. It's his cock we're after," she teases. "You look amazing. Let's see him deny you now."

She's seriously rooting for us and I'm terrified all I'm doing is setting myself up for heartbreak. "You're not wrong about the cock thing. My vibe is not cutting it these days. What about my hair?"

Chewing her lip, she studies my dark waves and arranges them in front of my shoulders. "Just like this. Mess it up a little at some point, give him something to fix. Fucker loves to fix things."

The fact that I'm such a mess makes me worry that's all the attraction is for him... him wanting to fix me. But I'm at the point where I can't focus on that right now. I'm in too deep, and if in the end, I get hurt... at least I enjoyed the journey. "Thanks, Dar. You think I can ride with you tonight?"

She grins mischievously. "Sure. Just go hide in the bathroom at closing and I'll conveniently forget I brought you."

"And I'll conveniently forgive you instantly," I joke. "Let's go. I learned how to make some new drinks I want to impress him with."

the night cap

The drive there is short, but Harvey's already waiting on a customer who must've shown up early when we walk in.

He seems to have dressed to impress me too because he's in a perfectly fitted plain black shirt that shows his bulging muscles. It has me weak as I make my way over with a smile. "Hey, boss. Can I stash my purse in your office tonight?"

"Of course, go ahead."

"You never let me keep my shit back there," Daria laughs, but Harvey doesn't miss a beat.

"You should know better than to bring valuables here."

I turn away without a word and go to hide it in his drawer, then go back to run my fingers along his back as I walk by. "Thank you."

He checks me out with a low hum and hungry eyes. She definitely knew what she was talking about with this outfit. "You're welcome," he says, quiet and full of promise. "You look good tonight, Calliope. You're not drinking, are you?"

"Maybe a couple. Am I allowed to?" I glance up at him through my lashes. "I've been good for a bit."

jensen

"That depends," he says flippantly, reaching under the bar to grab a glass. "How much blood do you want on your hands tonight?"

"Blood? What do you mean?"

The corner of his mouth quirks up. "You flirt when you drink. Judging by the last time you were here and how short that skirt is, I may end up in jail this time."

I hate how hard that makes me blush, but I can't help it. Him being protective is hot. "I'll be a good girl and keep the flirting to a minimum. Promise." I bump into him with my hip as I move to grab someone a couple of beers, but I can still feel his eyes on me.

Maybe I bend a little more than I need to.

When the crowd evens out, the playlist changes and I see Daria tossing me a wink while holding Harvey's phone. The switch from metalcore to pop makes Harvey drop what he's doing to come scold her, so I slip in front of him and start dancing to distract him. "You're not getting away that easy."

the night cap

His hand grips my hip. "This song is terrible," he mutters, yet his eyes darken as they drop to my waist, and I can tell he doesn't really care about anything else right now.

"Ed Sheeran can do no wrong. Just feel the music with me, handsome."

"Calliope," Harvey growls, thumb brushing the sliver of bare skin showing between my corset and skirt. "We have customers to wait on."

"They're enjoying the show. Why does my name sound so good when you say it and so blech when I do?"

"Because you're ridiculous." There's nothing but playfulness in his eyes, but this time he spins me toward the bar instead of back into his arms like the first time we danced. "I don't dance."

"Yeah, yeah, yeah, Mr. Grumps doesn't dance," I tease, refusing to release his hand until the last possible second. "You seem to *not* do a lot of things you do with me. Am I really that special?"

Some drunk guy yelling pulls Harvey's attention, but the answer is written all over his face. I am special. He just doesn't want to admit it yet.

jensen

That's okay. As long as you do one day, baby.

He mostly keeps to himself after that, focusing on the bar, the customers, and only stealing a couple hundred glances my way as the night progresses.

I feel every single one, like his eyes are a beacon shining so brightly my skin feels the warmth of his light. Even with my back turned, I feel his gaze and I can't help but smile every time.

I'm fucking hopeless.

I steal another dance before the night ends, then hide out in the bathroom as Daria sneaks out. Our plan is all working out so far. Now I need him to invite me upstairs and not miss the offer again.

"Hey, did Daria leave?" I ask, walking out and looking around like she might appear.

Harvey looks up from the register. "Yeah, she took off a couple of minutes ago."

"Oh shit, she was my ride." I fake a yawn. "I'll have to call someone. I'm beat, and this corset is killing me."

the night cap

His eyes flick down. "Do you *have* anyone to call? I don't want you getting in an Uber."

"I have four brothers... okay, technically only one that I can rely on to show up this late without complaint, but he had a date tonight and knowing him, it's still going on."

I yawn again, this one a little more real than the last, and that seems to do the trick.

Harvey jerks a shoulder up as he counts cash. "So stay with me."

"Yeah? Can I borrow your shower and a shirt?"

My heart speeds up as he licks his lips and hesitates, but he nods. "Of course."

"Thank you, hero." I toss him a wink before rushing into his office for my purse and making my way back. "You never said if you liked my resume."

If I didn't know better, I'd say he's trying not to smile. "It was as colorful as you are, so take that for what it's worth."

"I'll always be the sunshine to your grumpy, Sir."

I blow him a kiss and rush to his studio, yelling at myself the entire time up for blowing a kiss like a fucking dork, but the second his shower turns on, I wash all those fears and doubts down the drain.

I get out smelling like him, glad I stashed some clean panties in my purse before leaving earlier, and once I brush my teeth, I go through his drawers to find a shirt. He still isn't back, so I pick a faded Jack Daniels tee and moved over to the kitchen for some water. The click of his door makes me jump as I keep my back to him. "Thanks for this again, Harvey. This shirt is so comfortable."

He lets Dammit off his leash as he takes in the sight of me. "You can keep it. It looks better on you."

I'm so fucking happy he said that I nearly kiss him right here, but I spin around and offer him a smile instead. "Thanks, now I don't have to steal it."

"Hilarious." He hangs the leash and nods to the fridge. "You hungry or anything?"

"More snacky than hungry. You? Want me to make something?"

"Uh… yeah, if you want. I need to grab a shower, so just see what you can find," he offers. "There should be a few options in there."

I watch him go before rummaging through his fridge and cabinets, deciding on some nachos. There's leftover ground beef in the fridge, along with a can of my favorite nacho cheese and some top-notch tortilla chips. I top it off with some salsa, jalapeños and sour cream just as Harvey walks out with water clinging to his gorgeous, tattooed skin, murdering me in the process. His grey sweats hang low on his hips, and when I see the out-line of his bulge, I have to clench my legs. Fuck, I need him. He's playing dirty, just like I am.

"Nachos?"

"There will never be a time I say no to that," he says, gently caressing my hip as he slides behind me to grab plates for us. "Do you want to watch a rom-com while we eat?"

I take at least six seconds to recognize the deadpanned sarcasm, but I don't care. I spin around like that was the best thing he ever said and launch myself at him. "Really? You'd do that with me?"

jensen

He stiffens so hard I'm sure he's going to back out, but he wraps his arms around me and grunts in an uncomfortable agreement. "If you tell anyone, I'll fire you."

"Touchy," I tease, kissing his cheek once before turning around to grab the bowl. "Can we watch *Crazy, Stupid, Love?* It's funny, and streaming on Prime right now."

I move to his couch and grab the remote before he can respond, curling up and fighting a laugh at the dumbfounded look on his face. I have to hand it to Daria, she was right. He's eating out of the palm of my hand right now.

He joins me a little reluctantly, taking the blanket draped over the back of the couch and fixing it on my lap. "How long is this movie?"

"No clue. We don't have to finish it. The beginnings always have the funny parts and I can fill you in on the end."

I cuddle in close and eat a chip happily, beaming when he drapes his arm over my shoulder and leans in to steal a jalapeño slice. "We don't have to skip. I was curious. You were yawning downstairs."

the night cap

Busted.

"Yeah, the shower kinda woke me up, but I'm sure I'll be sleepy soon." I won't be, but I need to get him into that bed as soon as possible.

"Hmm." He settles in, kicking his feet up on the coffee table as Dammit comes over to beg. "Down, boy. Sit."

Dammit ignores him completely and jumps up on my side of the couch, tail wagging and tongue hanging out.

"Dammy just wants to watch the movie with us."

I turn to pout, then sneak him a chip without breaking eye contact with Harvey.

"So you're choosing to be a brat tonight?" he asks, voice low.

Fuck, it makes me squirm. "Do you want me to be a good girl?"

"That depends. Do you want to get spanked?"

I release a whimper — a fucking *whimper* — as I bite the shit out of my lip and clench my legs closed. I'd never wanted someone this bad in my entire life. Never. "I — wouldn't mind that."

The fuck did I just say?

jensen

His lips press against my forehead and he mumbles, "Watch your movie, sunshine," against my skin, and I nearly say no.

No, I don't want to watch this movie, I just want to watch your cock slide into my — oh god, I'm wet. Fuck.

I squeeze my legs tighter as Dammit leans in to sniff my lap, only this time I shove him away. "Not there, boy. That's a no-no area."

Harvey chuckles. "Sorry, I guess he really is my son."

I laugh with him, feeling a little more relaxed at his horrible joke. And it's only horrible because he hasn't stuck his face down there for me once.

When the food is gone, I set the bowl aside and go grab us each a bottle of water, holding one out for him while I fight the urge to crawl in his lap. "Let's go cuddle. We can finish the movie another time."

The tiny little smile on his face fades. "Calliope…"

"Harvey." I cross my arms. "It's just some harmless cuddling. It's been a long time for me." Years, but I doubt he actu-

the night cap

ally wants to know. It's no secret I like him, and I know cuddling is dangerous, but I hold my hand out anyway and brace for rejection. "Please?"

I see the silent fight in his head, but he stands and threads his fingers with mine. "How am I supposed to say no to you?"

"You're not," I say with a shrug, tugging him toward the bed with a smug smile. He may not be fucking me yet, but my plan is all coming together so far... I just have to hope those walls of his don't shoot right back up before the sun rises.

We both need this.

Chapter Ten:
The Pleasure

Callie

Melting into his chest feels so right, it hurts. I cling to him, inhaling his scent straight from the source and sighing at how delicious it is. "Thank you."

"Mmhm." He slips a hand down my body to grip my thigh, pulling it over his legs. "Just waiting to put up a wall of pillows."

"Don't you dare," I whisper, my fingers walking a trail down his torso until I splay them below his belly button. "No walls tonight."

His breath catches and his fingers curl against my back. "Calliope…"

the night cap

"Yes?" I tip my head up, noting the heat in his eyes before I take the biggest leap of my life and move to straddle him.

"Fuck." His restraint snaps. Tugging me down by my throat, he kisses me like he's starving and flips us over, slotting between my legs as his tongue coaxes my lips to part.

I open to him like he owns me, like this is what we've been doing all along, and I whimper as his tongue makes my toes curl.

"You're so fucking beautiful, Callie," he whispers, kissing down my shirt until his lips are ghosting over my shaking thighs.

My body twitches with his words, his touch, his fucking everything. I've wanted this since I saw him, and now that I actually know him, I want him even more. "Thank you, Harvey. I think you're beautiful, too."

Deft fingers pluck my panties off and toss them aside, but he doesn't look down yet. His eyes are on my borrowed shirt. "Sit up, baby. I want to see all of you."

jensen

"All my no-no areas?" I joke, sitting up so he can slip my shirt over my head.

"Don't say it like that, but yes." He drinks me in, slipping his hands over my belly and up my sides to cup my tits. "Goddamnit, you're gorgeous."

My back arches in desperation. "If I say it again, will you have to spank me?"

Chuckling darkly, he flips me onto my stomach. "I don't need a reason to do that, pretty girl." Broad hands slide over the expanse of my ass, squeezing and rubbing to warm the skin up. "I think I owe you a few already, hm?"

"Think so?" I wriggle under him, breathing harder than necessary as the anticipation builds. "I thought you liked when I brat."

"Oh, I wouldn't say that. I tolerate it when you act like a brat by picturing your gorgeous fat ass shaking for me," he mutters, spanking me just hard enough to make me gasp. He hisses, leaning down to bite the spot. "Better than I imagined."

"Fuck," I gasp. "Harder, baby."

He squeezes me hard, spreading my cheeks to spit on my ass, then spanks me twice. "One day, I'll spend more time doing this. I need your thighs around my head five fucking minutes ago. Roll over, gorgeous."

The mattress dips as Harvey slides off the bed to take his sweats off, and when I roll over and take in the sight of him, I groan. "Jesus, you're perfect. Your big hands aren't a myth."

My mouth waters as I stare at that thing, wondering if it'll even fit.

"Spread your legs." He climbs up to lie on his stomach, curling his arms under my thighs and exhaling hard. "How do you like to come, sunshine? What makes my girl tick?"

My hips roll, the '*my girl*' nearly makes me come all in itself. "Mostly clit, but I love fingers when I get close. You'll know when, baby."

"Then put me out of my misery, beautiful. I need to know what you sound like when you come."

His face disappears between my legs, his beard grazing my clenching thighs as his tongue explores. Every single swipe of it is akin to torture until he reaches my

jensen

desperate clit and pulls a moan straight from my core. "Harvey!"

"Good girl," he growls. "Taste so fucking good."

"Feels so good, please don't stop. Oh, fuck!"

He sucks my clit, moaning as his hands slide up my body. I feel him everywhere, my soaking pussy, my thighs, ass, and hips, but the best part is knowing this is only the beginning.

I feel that first one building quickly, my legs shaking as my breath hitches, and I struggle to mumble out, "Ba-by!"

Two skilled, thick fingers slide inside of me and curl just fucking right as his tongue flicks faster, and I fucking lose it. I gasp his name as I come all over his beard, my thighs clenching so hard around his head I'm sure he's going to complain, but he doesn't.

As he sits up, I see how hard he is. Hooded, hungry eyes stare down at me as his thumb takes the place of his tongue and his fingers continue to pump inside of me. "Now I want to watch. I've heard you and tasted you, but now I need to see it."

the night cap

"How are you real?" I ask as seriously as I can muster. "Really, how? You're perfect."

"For putting your pleasure first? Baby, your bar must be on the floor." His fingers move faster, backing off until he's applying just the right amount of pressure everywhere I need it and taking in the sight of my trembling body. "C'mon, pretty girl. Don't be shy."

He's not wrong. My bar is definitely pretty low because that's all I've ever had, so this is a whole new world. He'd kill me if I broke out in song, though. My fingers tug hard on his sheets as my back arches again, his name falling from my lips as I near the edge for a second time.

"It's selfish though," he rumbles, dropping down to kiss my belly, my chest. "Nothing turns me on more than seeing a gorgeous woman come apart for me." He's barely upright again in time to see me come hard, his fingers getting soaked by my arousal.

"Fuck!" I curse, unable to stop myself again. "Please... please get inside me."

"I can't, baby." A low grumble rattles his chest as he sucks his fingers clean, then lifts my leg to his shoulder to kiss my skin. "Believe it or not, I don't ever bring people up here. I don't have a condom."

Fucking gentleman.

With a sigh, I collapse onto his bed and send silent curses up into the sky, but we have to be smart about this. I'm pretty sure we're both negative and I religiously take my pill every morning, yet I know we have to wait. "Okay… fuck. Okay," I gasp. "I'll be patient."

"Good girl." He kisses my ankle, broad hands swiping down my thighs like he isn't done with me. "I'm still gonna make you come until you can't walk."

"What?" I whisper, my body tense all over and desperate again. It's been so long since I've allowed myself to be touched by a man, and even back then, they've never cared how many times I came. "And how about you? Do you get to come?"

He furrows his brows, slipping two fingers inside of me again. "My only concern tonight is you, Calliope. Let me rewrite everything you think you know about pleasure, and I promise, it'll be better than any orgasm you could give me. Now relax."

It's so easy to trust him, to know I'm safe here and that he'll never leave me wanting. Do I want him to have the same amount of pleasure as me? Absolutely. But there's something in his eyes that tells me he means this, that making me feel good brings him pleasure, and it's enough to have me fully on board. No one has ever put me first like this, no one. "Okay, Harvey. My body is yours… I trust you."

"That's my girl." Shifting with a slight smirk, he flattens one hand over my heart and twists his fingers inside me. "I want to feel your heartbeat kick up when I touch your clit again. Breathe for me."

My fingers curl against his sheets as I brace myself, releasing a deep breath for him as my body relaxes and opens to him. It makes him growl, a low, pleased sound as his eyes rake down my frame. There's no judgment there at my curves or fluff, just sheer arousal as my heartbeat steadily speeds up instead of evens out.

jensen

I need to come, and the way his fingers move inside of me is tantalizing yet not enough — but that's his plan. "You want it, don't you, pretty girl?" His thumb just barely grazes my clit, making me jerk. "You need it?"

"Yes!" I gasp. "Please, baby. I need it, I need it."

I can't even find it in me to be embarrassed by how quickly I beg, because my Harvey doesn't make me wait. His fingers splay over my chest as his thumb presses down on my clit, and my heartbeat goes insane as I soak his fingers and forget to breathe entirely.

"Good girl, that's it. Come all over my fingers. More, pretty girl. Don't stop now."

He moves faster, driving his fingers deeper, curling them just right to have me crying out and singing his name like a song. "S-So good! Oh my god, how are you real?!"

"Fuck," he growls, working me through it and pulling his fingers out so suck them clean. "Are you okay? I want more."

the night cap

I can see it in his eyes. This isn't the guy who left me grumpy, impersonal notes. This is a man obsessed, a man with one singular goal in mind. I truly don't know if I can handle more, but he needs it, and for some reason, I know he can pull more from me. So I nod. "You can have whatever you need, baby."

"God, you're perfect." He drops forward to kiss me, the taste and scent of my pussy heavy on his beard as he licks into my mouth like he needs me to understand how much he means it, and I do. As he kisses down my body, worshiping every extra pound and insecurity, I whimper, realizing in that moment how much I've needed this.

Needed him.

I don't ever want to go back — no other man can compare, I just know it.

"Harvey!"

"It's okay, baby." He bites my thigh, settling between my legs again. "Just pull me off when you can't take it anymore."

That insistent, glorious tongue finds my clit again, the overstimulation becoming the best kind of torture I've ever experienced. "Oh f-fuck!"

jensen

I yank on his hair to get him to stop, but he fights my grip and growls against my throbbing pussy as his fingers curl in my hips. His mouth works faster, pulling another orgasm from me that has tears spilling from my eyes and my body trembling under him. "I can't! Harvey!"

He glares up at me, mumbling, "That was fast," then carefully, slowly licks the mess up before sliding off the bed and holding out a hand. "You're okay. Come with me. You need water and a bathroom break."

"My legs are jelly," I mumble sleepily, letting him pull me to my feet. "I've never come that many times before."

"Your bar really is on the floor." Strong arms sweep me off my feet, carrying me the few feet to the bathroom. He puts me right on the toilet, then kisses my head and disappears to the kitchen, coming back with a bottle of water just as I'm flushing. While I drink like I'm dying of thirst, Harvey wets a washcloth and nods down at my thighs. "Spread, pretty girl."

I stare at him in awe after I do as told, watching him clean me like I'm someone special in his life, and for now… I let my-self believe him. He's proven to me that I am. "Thank you."

I reach out and touch his face gently, seeing the way he nearly flinches at it. It's not in a bad way, it just… reminds me he's been alone for a long time.

"Don't thank me, Calliope. Just come back to bed."

"Only if you promise cuddles," I say with a soft smile, leaning in to kiss his lips once to show him I'm still here. He's not alone anymore.

He grunts, shaking his head to deny me, yet once he's got me back in his shirt and comfortable under the blankets, the big grump pulls me to him and whispers, "Shh. Not a word."

I don't say anything. I hum a noise that lets him hear and feel how happy I am, because sometimes words aren't needed to express happiness. These cuddles say it all.

Chapter Eleven: The Slip

Harvey

Slowly, I sip my coffee and stare at the absolute bitchface Dammit is giving me. I'm scared to move, scared to speak, scared to do anything at all for fear that Calliope might wake up and I'll have to deal with the consequences of my actions.

I fucked up last night.

So, so badly.

It started with that damn kiss in my office two weeks ago. I knew I shouldn't do it, but I was too adrenaline-filled and chaotic to make rational decisions and the way she bit her bottom lip drew me in like a siren's song.

the night cap

And stupid, foolish me should've known I'd never be satisfied with one kiss.

I take another drink of my coffee, ignoring the soft sounds of her snoring in my bed as Dammit judges me.

She'd been so perfect for me last night. Everything I've ever wanted. Women always claim they want a man who cares about their pleasure, but in my experience, it's got an asterisk attached to it. Most can't comprehend that a man can exist solely to please them. That they have nothing to be embarrassed about, they have nothing to fear. No orgasmic quotas to fill in order to be needed, wanted, cherished. I couldn't care less if I come as long as my partner knows exactly how important she is.

It's something my ex could never grasp, no matter how many times I tried to explain it, and then Calliope Marino comes in with her obnoxious pants and cheery personality and gets it the very first time.

God, where has she been all my life?

jensen

Dammit whines, so I reach down to pet his head. "Shh, boy. Let me enjoy this for a few more minutes, yeah?"

And that's all it will be. Just a few more minutes, because I can't. I just fucking can't. I feel the fear squeezing my chest and making it hard to breathe already, and it's only been a few weeks. If I let her in and she leaves, I don't know what I'll do.

This is why I've kept to myself. Why I've stayed single despite all the blind dates people have set me up on, all the worthy women who have come my way. None of them has been as worthy as her, and that's what fucking terrifies me.

She's my employee now. I knew better.

Standing, I go to refill my coffee cup and see her sitting up in bed when I turn back around.

Here we go.

"Good morning," I say as gently as I can.

"Morning." She smiles wide and sleepy at me while getting out of bed and heading into my bathroom, giving me a few more minutes to get my shit together. When she comes back out, she looks more awake. That smile hasn't left her face. "How long have you been up?"

The kiss she places on my cheek nearly ruins my resolve. God, she's so beautiful, it's painful. "A while," I hedge. "How'd you sleep?"

"Better than I have in… ever." She laughs, pouring herself some coffee, but I see something change in her as she looks at me again. Like she can feel something is coming. "You?"

"Good." It's the truth, just not the whole truth. "So you're not angry with me?"

"Of course not. Should I be?" she asks in confusion.

Not yet, but you're probably about to be.

I take a moment to really make sure I know what I'm doing, but the truth is, I don't. Calliope has turned me inside out and upside down in like a month, but old habits die hard. I remember all too well the look on puppy-Dammit's face when my ex walked out and he realized she wasn't coming back, and as I watch the grown-up version in front of me wag his tail and run over to Callie begging to be pet, I realize I'm not just protecting myself here.

I'm protecting him too, and if I'm being completely honest, Callie herself.

She deserves someone who will go all-in with her, not constantly have one foot out the door because they're a coward. It's not fair to her.

Finally, I shake my head a little. "I'd be mad at me if I were you."

"Why?" Her nervous gaze locks on mine again as she stands, Dammit whimpering like he wasn't done with her yet, and maybe also to protect her from the pain I'm about to cause. "What is it, Harvey?"

He always has known me better than anyone.

"Do you remember how I explained to you I don't date my employees or people who frequent my bar?" I ask, hoping that maybe she'll convince me I'm nuts. It's an unfair thing to put on her and I know that, but I've always been a self-aware asshole. "That it's a hard line for me?"

"How could I forget?" She sets her coffee aside, understanding where this is going. "Thought I was special, I guess.

the night cap

You trying to politely tell me you regret what happened between us last night?"

"You don't have to regret something to know it shouldn't happen again," I explain, willing her to believe me. "I'll never regret making you feel good, Callie."

"Thanks?" It's a question, and she's already shutting down like I expected her to. "So it won't happen again. That's what you're saying? Because I'm a temporary employee of yours?" Her hazel eyes water slightly, but I can tell she refuses to cry. She's too stubborn for that.

What the fuck am I doing? Hurting her to spare myself? "I'm sorry," is all I can say. It's not enough, and honestly, I don't know what I'm even apologizing for. Leading her on? Being too constipated to have an honest discussion about it? For being weak?

All of it.

"Me too," she hisses, moving past me to get her clothes on, but she rounds on me before she leaves, my shirt still clinging to her body. "Fine. I've tried here, Harvey, I really have. It's you who hasn't. Blame the fact that I was a regular at your bar even though it had only been like three visits. Blame the fact that I'm a temporary worker, but you and I both know your problem with this is so much deeper than that, and I'm not going to stand around and wait for you to break my heart. I can't, and if you want to keep living in the past, you go ahead. I won't be there."

She leaves before I can respond, and I deserve it, even though I feel like I'm as hurt now as I'd be in five months if she left then. How is it we always end up writing self-fulfilling prophecies when it comes to trying to protect ourselves?

All I've done now is hurt her, hurt myself, hurt Dammit who's staring at the door with the same wounded, abandoned look he had when my ex walked out. But this time, I can't blame the woman who did the leaving.

This one's on me, and nobody fucking else.

At nine o'clock, I crumple the schedule up into a ball and toss it into the trash. Callie's shift started an hour ago and she's not here, which tells me she meant what she said earlier. Thoroughly. I went from having her in every way to not having any part of her, and that's on me — meaning I can't put it on Daria either. I can't call her in here to help me when it's my fault that I'm about to deal with the Saturday night slam alone.

But fuck, I forgot how hard it is to bartend alone on a weekend.

By midnight, I'm six seconds from splitting someone's lip. The next person who snaps at me for not getting them a drink fast enough is going to end up in the goddamn morgue, and I'm half tempted to close early so that doesn't happen.

I wouldn't do well in prison.

I'm just about to call it quits when Daria walks through the door looking madder than I am, and I've got a defense half-cocked and ready to go when she steps behind the bar and angrily washes her hands. "Why the hell didn't you call me?" she snaps. "I'd have been here hours ago if you would've."

Whoa. That isn't what I expected.

Popping the cap on a beer, I slide it to the next asshole and hurry to close a tab,

jensen

talking as I type. "Because. I wasn't going to call you in on your night off, especially since you clearly don't know why I'm here alone."

She hits me with the towel she's using to dry her hands. "Oh, I know why, you idiot. Callie called me. But just because I think you're the dumbest, sorriest, meanest son of a bitch to ever walk the earth right now doesn't mean I'm not going to come help you out when you need it. I'm offended you'd even think that. Now go swap the kegs I know are out and take five minutes to wipe that ridiculous look off your face. I've got this."

Shooing me out of the way, she takes over serving people and allows me time to sneak to the back. That woman deserves a big fat raise for putting up with me and I know that, but I can't help but wonder what the hell Calliope said to her to make her yell at me that way.

Was I really that mean?

I tried to be gentle, but as two of the former patrons of my bar can now attest, 'gentle' has never been something I've been very good at. I'm 6'2 and built like a tank with hands the size of fucking base-

121

the night cap

ball mitts and all the grace of a gorilla. And my demeanor… there's a reason my life turned out the way it did. I've never been gentle. Never been soft. Never been anything resembling worthy, but I tried with Calliope harder than I've tried at anything in years.

It just wasn't good enough, because I wouldn't fucking let it be good enough.

Maybe Daria's right.

Chapter Twelve: The Pain

Callie

For a few days, I sit around my house feeling sorry for myself and ridiculously sad. I feel sad for everyone involved actually, and the weight it is almost too heavy to bear. Daria for having to pick up my slack at the bar. My brothers, who I've ignored. My old boss I groveled to when I begged for my job back. Dammit for not saying goodbye. But most of all, I feel sad for Harvey, because I know I'll never understand the way he feels inside and why he doesn't feel worthy of love. In fact, my heart breaks for him every time I allow myself to think of him and no matter how hard I try, I can't stop.

the night cap

I focus on what I have to do tomorrow to help, nerves tingling under my skin as I imagine walking into Wrapz with my head held high and my dignity intact. Sounds impossible from here, but I don't really have a cho — "What the hell, Cals!"

"Ah!" I scream at the top of my lungs, launching a pillow to my left in fear and making my youngest brother put his fists up like he's ready to fight a burglar. Only in my mind, *he's* the burglar.

"Xander! You scared the shit out of me!"

"I scared *you?"* he yells right back, his hands finally unclenching at his sides. "You haven't said a word in two days." I frown at him before I hide back under my blankets, ignoring him when he climbs right up beside me and sighs. "Adrian is in the kitchen, but for right now, it's just me. What happened?"

"Nothing," I lie, knowing how pathetic I probably look to him. "I've just been tired."

"What's his name?"

I pull the covers off my head and glare at him. "Why are you assuming it—"

jensen

"Cut the shit, Cals. I know you when you're tired, when you're angry, when you're sad. I know you've never been this way before though, so that leaves one thing I've never seen you as: heartbroken."

How can I be heartbroken if I never had the opportunity to love?

"It was over before it got to that point," I admit. "Actually, I don't think it ever even began… I just fooled myself into believing it did."

Xander's jaw ticks, his hands clenching again like he wants to walk out right now and find the man I'm talking about. "So he led you on?"

I lay my head back down and toss an arm over my eyes. "No, he didn't. He was pretty clear about where he stood from the beginning, actually. This can't be blamed on him, Xan. I practically threw myself at him and he was too much of a nice guy not to catch me… even if all he was catching me for was to put me on my feet. He was never meant to be mine. I was just stupid and thought maybe I was the exception."

the night cap

"I don't fully understand what you're saying, but I don't care if you think he shouldn't be blamed. Who is he? Give me a name."

"No," I argue. "I won't tell you anything else if you're going to go all *big bro* on me. Either be here for me or don't."

"What's going on?" Adrian mumbles around a PB&J sandwich, walking in with a couple more in his hands for us, too.

I'm not hungry, but I know for a fact that neither of them will leave until I've eaten, so I take one and sit up. They both chuckle at my bedhead but I don't even attempt to fix it. They're my brothers and they've seen me at my absolute worst, just like I've seen them in every imaginable state of disarray. "I have a crush on a guy that will never be mine," I admit as he climbs on my bed, too. "XanMan was being protective as always, but I won't say who he is. He didn't do anything wrong."

"If you're sad, then he did something wrong," he replies, and Xander waves a hand at him like he just said the most obvious thing ever.

"Listen, I love you both, but this is exactly why I haven't said anything. I don't need you guys to beat anyone up. We're adults now, and believe it or not, I'm not perfect."

They share an over-the-top surprised look before Adrian pulls out his phone and pretends to broadcast live. "Breaking news: this just in, Calliope Marino has just admitted she is not, in fact, perfect. You heard that right, folks. She is *not* perfect."

Xander snatches his phone to chime in, "Mark this day down on your calendars as members of government have made this day a national holiday."

"I hate you guys." I take a bite of my sandwich and turn away from them, but I feel better than I have in days, so I have to give these two idiots that much.

At least I'll always have them.

I walk out for my break with my phone in my hand, already hating this place all over again, but I push those feelings aside as I call Daria back. "Hey, sorry. I was working. How are you?"

"Working? Where?" she asks, her tone curious.

the night cap

"Wrapz." I fake a gag. "I didn't have a choice, but I already decided I'm going to look for a job I actually enjoy this time. This is temporary."

Daria releases an accusatory hum. "You *had* a job you actually enjoyed, remember?"

How could I forget? "I know."

She can hear the lace of sadness in my tone. I know she can. "You ready to talk about that yet?"

"I mean, what do I say? I was falling for a man that will never feel the same. I had to leave before I broke my own heart." Even though it still feels like I didn't dodge a bullet at all, only stepped into its trajectory.

"That's a good place to start. Especially since I don't believe you're the only one hurting here."

I hate thinking about how I hurt him, too. I know I did, but he also expected me to, so he kept walls up I wasn't capable of building for myself. Not before this, anyway. "How is he?"

"Probably exactly how you'd imagine. He's grouchier than ever before, sadder too, and he hardly talks to anyone. All he does is keep busy working inside and outside the office and then he just goes upstairs."

She's right, that's exactly what I imagined. It still hurts to hear it. "I'm sorry."

"For what? You don't have to apologize to me, girl."

It actually wasn't to her, it was to him. She's just the only person around to hear it. "I know. I feel shitty about it all. I should have stayed away."

Daria sighs like I'm an idiot and I have no argument there. "No, you gave him a chance and he came out behind those walls more than I've ever seen him."

My eyes sting with unshed tears, at how she viewed him during our short time together — or whatever we were. "I wish it was enough."

"Me too."

We steer the conversation from our sadness over Harvey and me, and she tells me that a guy she's been talking to for a while finally asked her to be his girl. Never one to let a guy off the hook

the night cap

that easily, she told him she'd let him know, but I think she's going to say yes.

At least I hope she does, because someone in this story deserves a happy ending, and she deserves it just as much as the rest of us.

Chapter Thirteen: The Drunk

Harvey

"Don't," I mutter to Daria as she opens her mouth. She's just setting her phone down after shooting off a text, and based on the look on her face, she's about to yell at me again for hurting Calliope. "I don't need to hear it right now. We're about to open and half the liquor bottles are still empty from last night. I don't need a lecture."

Flipping me off, she swaps the pour spout to a new Jack Daniels bottle. That one was my fault. "I wasn't going to lecture you, but it's good to know that she's been gone for two weeks and you're still

the night cap

incapable of thinking about anything but her."

How the hell is that a good thing?

All I do is grunt in response and turn our computer on to give it time to boot up. Clearly, Daria *was* about to lecture me, because nothing else comes out of her mouth until she yells that she's about to flip the sign and unlock the door. For once, I'm grateful that tonight should be slow. Normally busy evenings help give me something else to focus on and I can't complain about the money, but tonight, I just want to shut my fucking brain off and have a drink with my regulars.

They're the closest things I have to friends.

Red walks in like clockwork at a half past seven with his favorite leather jacket slung over his shoulder and his best friend behind him. Sam's been coming here nearly as long as Red has and has spent almost twice as much money, so I nod a greeting to them both and pour their usuals. "Anticipating a slow night, so let's drink," I say, grabbing a beer this time just in case I'm wrong. "If you two promise to just be cool and have a good time, your drinks are on the house tonight."

"Hell," Sam exclaims. "That's all we ever do and you always make us pay, Pierce. That's some shit."

Red smacks him, coughing a laugh. "You fuckwit, hasn't anyone ever told you not to insult the man who's letting you drink for free?"

Oh, yeah. This was a good choice.

I listen to the two of them bicker until my beer is out and Daria's side-eyeing me as I take another. "What?" I challenge. "It's my bar, isn't it?"

She purses her lips and nods. "Sure is, boss. I guess you have more of a right to make dumbass decisions here than any-one."

Cold, but true enough that I don't pay her any mind. I've had this bar for almost five years and I've hardly ever had a drop of my own alcohol. I've never set foot down here drunk, never did a goddamn thing to get myself in trouble. Well... ex-cept maybe assaulting two of my patrons, but they both had it coming and then some. That second son of a bitch is lucky

the night cap

all I did was break the hand he used to grab my girl.

No, she's *not* my girl.

Clearly I need to drink a little faster.

"Sammy, why don't you put something good on the jukebox?" I ask, trying to keep the mood light as a couple more frequent fliers make their way in and grab a booth toward the back. "Something loud."

"It's all loud, son," he argues, groaning as he pushes his old bones up off the barstool. When the song changes a few moments later and I recognize the beginning of "Whipping Post," I have to hand it to the guy. He's got just about as good of taste in music as he does in alcohol, but the jackass opens his mouth again before I can give him too much credit. "So where's your girlfriend?"

I ignore him.

"Hey! Earth to Harvey," he prods. "I thought I was the deaf one around here. Where's your girlfriend been?"

Draining my second beer, I toss it in the recycling bin and grab a third. "Don't have one, Sammy. How long have you known me?"

jensen

"Long enough to know you've got the hots for that pretty little thing you had runnin' around here a few weeks ago." He points a crooked, wrinkled finger at me, and for the first time, I wonder how old he actually is. "Now where'd ya hide her? She was nice. Used to put a little lime slice in my gin for me. You never give me no limes."

Jesus Christ.

I flip open the lid to our garnish cooler and grab a lime, shoving it on the rim of his gin and tonic. "There. You've got a lime. Happy?"

Red steals it almost instantly and throws it at me, bouncing it off my chest and onto the floor. "Alright, you little shit. Free drinks or no free drinks, you're breaking your own rule. Now where's the girl? It's a simple question."

Anger flares in my gut that I'm not expecting. Sadness, sure. Pain, yeah. Guilt, definitely. But anger? That one's new. "She quit," I yell, unable to stop myself. "You happy? Calliope quit. She's not coming back, so quit fucking asking about her."

the night cap

Silence fills the bar until Daria scoffs loudly.

"What?" I snap, too far gone to give a shit. "You got something to say? She quit, it's the truth."

"Yeah, because you were being a dick!" she retorts. "You've always been a little rough to deal with, Harvey, but this is ridiculous. You're yelling at your friends, getting drunk at your own bar, snipping at me all the damn time when I'm the only one left in your life that cares enough to help you out. Callie *didn't* quit. You forced her out of here because you're too far up your own ass to see how much you need her. How perfect she is for you. You know she texted me earlier to ask me if you're okay?" She laughs bitterly. "I can't imagine why the hell she still cares at this point, cause I sure don't. Maybe she had the right idea, leaving you to drown all by yourself."

I stand there, too stunned to say anything at all back to her as she throws her hands up in the air and marches toward the back. Red and Sammy both stand, dropping twenties on the bar top like I didn't tell them their tabs were on me,

136

and I still don't know what the hell to say to them as Red puts his jacket on. "Sounds like you should call her, Harvey. Never seen you like this, but I agree with the lady. Can't say I'm a real big fan of it."

They leave me standing there like an asshole with a wet spot on my shirt and something suspiciously close to tears welling in my eyes. I try to keep myself safe, I fail. I try to be happy, I fail. I'm my own worst enemy, and the problem is that now, I'm bringing everyone else down with me.

What the hell did she see in me, anyway?

Thank god I live upstairs.

Stumbling, it takes me three tries to unlock my door, and suddenly I know how Calliope must've felt the first couple of times she came up here. Walking through my front door feels foreign as hell as I try to close the right door — shit, there's only supposed to be one of those. Why are there two?

the night cap

"Shit, Dammit. Close the door," I slur, seconds from throwing up. Vague memories of closing the bar early and getting drunk to a blues playlist are a little too fresh in my mind, which is annoying. I got blackout drunk for the first time in years to forget about things, not have them bouncing around and making me even more nauseous.

Swallowing hard, I get the door locked and kick my shoes off before remembering Dammit hasn't gone out in hours. I'm half tempted to just let him do his business wherever the hell he pleases, but then I remember he's a ninety-pound Akita and that's a god-awful idea.

I down some water and throw a pot of coffee on, then piss my brains out twice before I think I'm stable enough to walk him without accidentally wandering into traffic, and the chilly night air does wonders to sober my ass up a bit.

But with sobriety comes sadness. I'm in that bullshit middle stage now between blackout and having fun where everything hurts and the world seems like it was designed by a sadist who enjoys seeing people in pain. I'm pretty sure I can ignore it and just go to sleep, until we get back upstairs and my bastard dog waltzes straight toward the corset Callie left here the day she stormed out and lies on it like a pillow. It's my fault for not having the balls to pick it up and put it away somewhere, but fuck. I didn't need that tonight.

"C'mon, boy. Up," I grumble, rubbing the back of his neck and gently trying to move him off of it. He growls at me, moving more on top of it, and I give up. "Whatever. Lay on it, then. Hope it pokes you."

Instantly, I feel bad. Daria was right. I've been insufferable lately, and it isn't fair to anyone involved.

"Sorry, Dam. C'mere." Grunting, I lay down with him on the floor and wrap an arm around him, petting his belly. "Your dad's a dick, you know that? But it's okay. I'm gonna find a way to fix it all, I promise. No more drinking, no more snapping. We're gonna be alright."

Down here with his warmth pressed against me, sleep pulls me under quickly, and I reach a state of semi-consciousness that allows me to believe that I just might do it. I just might make everything okay.

I've gotta at least try.

Chapter Fourteen: The Brothers

Callie

It's been a month since I quit Harvey's and I still can't convince myself it was a fever dream. It'd be easier if I could, if I could trick my mind into thinking Harvey was a figment of my imagination or a book boyfriend — but I can't. The books I read always have happy endings, and even with as perfect a boyfriend as I know he *could've* been, our story did not end the way my books do. So no, he'd be better off as imaginary, or maybe as the man that haunts my dreams. The one that only visits on restless nights and leaves me alone for days on end.

the night cap

Instead, he's a real part of my past, and him being real means the pain is also real. I hate that I can still feel his kiss on my lips, that our single night together lives rent-free in my mind and every time I feel myself getting turned on, all I see is him between my thighs. I haven't gotten off since that day, and the more time that passes, the worse my personal torture becomes.

Stop thinking about stuff like that, Callie. It's your niece's birthday party today.

It's also the first time I've left my house on a Saturday, so I take my time to do my makeup and hair nicer than I need to for this, but toss on some stretchy, pink leggings and a black blouse to balance it out and then head over to my oldest brother's home.

The lawn is decked out in purple and teal balloons, the mermaid theme strong before I even make it to the porch and see the giant cut-out adorning the wall. Rosalie is turning six though, so I really didn't expect anything different. I don't know a lot of the people here very well. Gio's wife Nicole has two sisters who both have multiple kids, so the amount of cousins I see running around makes me smile. Who knows when we'll add to that on our side?

"Calliope!" Leo calls loudly, running over to hug me tightly with his husband, Amari, right on his heels. They introduce me to his niece as well, but she's already running around with all the other kids and fitting in nicely.

Everyone is there except Adrian, who messaged the group chat that he'd be here in five minutes a half an hour ago, but we're used to that. Five minutes in *Adrian* is always at least forty-five, so we have another fifteen before Xander gets worried and calls him.

Bianca spots me before Rosalie, running over quickly to jump into my arms and beat her sister in a race to me. I hug and lift them both, realizing then I probably won't be able to do this with them soon with how fast they're growing. Kids really do grow up too fast.

"I have so many presents!" Rosey yells excitedly. "Do you think one is a real mermaid?"

the night cap

I hate to be the one to break it to her, so I don't. "Maybe! I think if anyone found one for you, it was Leo."

She turns to him with wide eyes, and I almost feel guilty for passing that torch to him. He has a very mature conversation about how mermaids belong in the sea, and the teacher in him shines pretty brightly as he levels with her. They handle it so well I feel a little less guilty for a second, so I move on to say hi to Nicole and her family. Before I know it, I'm back with my brothers and taking bets on when Adrian will arrive.

"I say he walks in any minute," Gio says confidently. "He won't miss the food."

We laugh at how true that is just as the door opens and the man himself walks in. Our laughs all taper off when we see his face and the evidence that he was in a fight yesterday, and I rush over to grab his arm and tug him over to our little corner. "What happened?"

For a moment. I think of how protective he and Xander were about Harvey, but there's no way he found out who he is and went there without Xan, so I force myself not to stress over that and wait for a response.

"I knew you guys were going to get all weird about it," he grumbles. "Wouldn't have come if it wasn't for Rosey."

"And food," Gio adds, making Adrian chuckle and shrug his shoulders.

"Whatever. You know the girl I was seeing? Leah?" We all nod, even though I'm pretty sure none of us have met her. "Apparently, she had a boyfriend."

My jaw drops. No words come to me as Xander speaks up and proves to me that at least one of us has, in fact, met her. "I knew she was shady! Remember I told you I saw her at a restaurant with some dude?"

"Yeah, but she swore it was her cousin, and she told me about it before you did, so I believed her."

"She only told you because I said something to her. She knew I'd tell you," he argues.

"It's whatever, we weren't serious or anything, anyway. The point is, she actually *was* in a serious relationship and knew he was going to propose soon, so she claims she wanted to feel free before she was tied down. She said she knew I was the kind of guy that wouldn't take a relationship seriously, so I was a safe bet. But he found out and showed up at my fucking apartment."

"What a bitch!" I whisper sharply, looking around to make sure no kids are too close. "Both of them. He can't blame you for *her* being a cheater."

"I think he wanted someone else to blame, honestly. Like I said, it's whatever. We both got some aggression out and went on with our lives. I told her to lose my number. When's the food going to be ready?" He rubs his stomach like he's been waiting for this all day, making Gio laugh.

"It's already ready. So you don't want us to all go kick his ass?"

Adrian shakes his head without hesitation. "If you think my face looks bad, you should see his. I took care of it. How long has it been since you two have been in a fight, anyway?"

My two oldest brothers look offended at the insinuation, but we all know it's been a long time for them both. Leo scoffs. "Hey, once a brawler, always a brawler."

"Bullshit," Xander disagrees, but he says it so loud Nicole's mom gasps from across the room and he tries to hide behind the rest of us. "Oops."

"Yeah, *oops*." Giovanni swings back to hit him in the nuts, and luckily for both of them, the cusses that leave his mouth after that are too low to be heard by anyone but us. While he doubles over in pain, my oldest brother continues, "What Leo means is we had our fighting days and if we ever needed to, we can be that again."

I think about the stories they've told me and how hard Leo had it growing up knowing he was gay, but these days, he's definitely the happiest out of all of us. I'm just happy he found Amari when he did. They're perfect for each other.

We all make our way over to fill up on cheese pizza and cake, then move outside to relax on Gio's porch as the kids enjoy the last couple hours of daylight. The party thins out while we're out there until eventually it's just us and the sun has long since set, and as the music plays and Otis

the night cap

Redding comes on, I feel a clench in my chest that reminds me I'm far from over the man I'm not allowed to want.

I'm happy my brothers don't drill me more about why I've been so sad. If they did tonight, especially with that song playing, I might actually cry. It's the last thing they need to see, and I refuse to end this amazing family time on a sad note. We needed this time together, and when they all start tossing around memories, I'm able to bury that sadness for a little while longer and live in the moment with them. A piece of me wishes they could have met him, but the rest of me knows this is for the best. I already don't know if I'll ever stop missing him or mourning what could have been, and if I'd brought him into my family — or into any more of my life than I already had — who knows if I ever would have gotten over him.

I already have the feeling I won't.

Chapter Fifteen: The Tulip

Harvey

"I'm sorry."

Daria eyes me like she's not sure whether or not to believe me, but nods all the same. "Mmhm. It's not me you have to apologize to, Harvey. I've dealt with your mood swings enough over the years to know you don't really mean it when you lash out, but others might not."

Calliope. Sam. Red.

"I know," I admit. "I've already sent Sam and Red apology bottles of my best gin, but I need a little help with Calliope. I don't know how to reach her."

the night cap

She opens her mouth to retort, then pauses. "You don't have her phone number?"

"No." Embarrassment creeps up my spine. "I never needed it. She was always just… here. I think she put it on her resume, but I apparently shredded that the night I got hammered. I've been looking for it for two weeks and it's gone."

"So, what do you want me to do about it? I don't feel comfortable giving you her number if she didn't give it to you herself."

"I understand your hesitation, but—"

"No buts, Harvey. I'm not going to just give you her number." Daria sighs, reaching across the table to squeeze my hand. "I think you've hurt her — and yourself — enough."

That's a fucking understatement. "You're not hearing me. You're right, I have hurt us both enough, and that's the whole point. I've spent my adult life running from emotions because I married a woman I had no business marrying in the first place. I didn't love her, Dar. I thought I did. But the truth is… Heather leaving didn't hurt half as bad as watching Calliope walk out my door. I've been a colossal idiot, but I can't get her out of my head. Tell me how to find her."

Her wild purple hair becomes the only thing I can see as she launches herself across the table to hug me, startling the shit out of me. I barely catch her in time to stop her from toppling onto the ground. "I'm not giving you her number," she repeats. "But I will tell you she got her old job back. If you remember where that is because you actually paid attention to her, then it won't be that hard to find her yourself and grovel until she takes you back."

Grovel.

It sounds so... traumatizing, but something tells me that Daria's right yet again. Calliope Marino deserves more than just a passing apology from me, and if I have to check every Wrapz in the tri-county area until I find which one she works at... I will.

The first Wrapz I check is at the corner of Fifth and Melrose. There's no recognition on the manager's face when I say her name, so I drive to the one on McDonell Drive.

This guy definitely recognizes her name but insists she doesn't work there, and I spent ten minutes trying to convince him I'm not a psycho before he finally admits he went to high school with her, but she doesn't work there.

What a fucking waste of time.

The third employee I grill threatens to call the cops on me, and the fourth tells me she's worked a few shifts there, but it's not her home store, yet won't tell me where her home store is.

Why the hell do we need so many of these places in a relatively small town?

Pulling up a map, I study the last three locations because the next person to tell me they don't know her might just get on my bad side. There has to be one that makes more sense than the others — and ultimately, I decide to try the one on Nestor and Camino. It's close enough to my bar that it makes sense she'd have heard of it, but far enough away that it explains why she couldn't find a ride home those first few nights. If she lives close to it… this has to be it.

jensen

Now I have to hope she's actually working.

Bracing myself, I throw on a metalcore playlist and drive the fifteen minutes across town, then spot her Volvo in the parking lot.

Thank fucking god. Everything's going to be fine.

Parking quickly, I grab the single purple tulip that hasn't utterly given up on life during this drive and walk in before I can lose my nerve. I don't see her right away, which just gives me time to talk myself out of this. She made it clear she didn't want to be around, so what if that hasn't changed?

What if I can't make her see?

It's then, of course, that she walks out from the back. I watch her note the ingredients they're low on and disappear once again, but even in those few seconds, I don't miss the way her energy has changed. I don't feel the sunshine radiating off of her like before, especially when she walks back out with a frown and a hairnet and starts wrapping burritos. She hated this part of her job; she told me as much.

the night cap

Suddenly her gaze snaps up like she can feel me standing there and her mouth parts in a gasp I can't hear, but she stays there utterly frozen.

"Hi," I offer as the sight of her threatens to undo me. "You're a hard person to track down, Calliope."

Suddenly, the tulip in my hand doesn't seem sufficient, but I hold it out anyway and hope she understands the metaphor. This is me, handing her my heart.

She stares a few minutes longer like she isn't sure if she's gone crazy, then tells them she's going on her break. She doesn't say anything at all until we're outside, and even then I can see her walls are up, but at least she took the flower. "You were looking for me?"

"Mmhm. I think I traumatized a few people at the other Wrapz around here. Oops."

She fights a smile at that and wins. "Yikes. So… why?"

Her eyes meet mine, and now that I'm here, all the words that made sense a bit ago get jumbled.

"Red and Sammy keep asking about you," I say. "All our regulars miss you."

jensen

"Oh," she breathes, exhaling hard as she breaks our stare. "They'll move on. Not like I was around long, anyway."

"And Daria," I add quickly. "I know you two still talk, but she misses having you around. Don't think she enjoys the job as much without you."

She finally looks at me. "Let me guess, Dammit too?"

Studying her face, it's clear there's no longing there, no hope or sadness or excitement or love. Just... cold, and I have to wonder if that's how I looked to her the day she walked out on me. "Yeah," I mumble, no longer sure what I'm doing here. "He's been waiting by the door for you every night."

It's then I see the sadness. I'm so enraptured by it I don't even notice she's handing me back my flower. "Almost everyone then. But not enough. Bye, Harvey."

"Calliope," I call as she walks away, but she doesn't turn around. She leaves me standing there with this stupid flower and my heart somewhere in a puddle on the ground, not looking back.

I guess that's that, then.

the night cap

As I drive home in a daze, I don't even bother turning the radio on in my car. The thoughts in my head are loud enough as it is.

She's right, what I just did wasn't good enough. Women like Calliope Marino deserve more than a single bent flower and enough stalking to give cause for a restraining order.

They deserve the world and a man better than me to stand beside them.

What was I thinking?

Some little voice reminds me I was thinking I was falling in love as I tromp up the stairs to my apartment. I was thinking I've been lonely, that I was finally tired of being miserable and alone when all I had to do to change that was admit that Callie already got under my skin. I didn't even have to let her in… I just had to admit she already was.

"C'mon, Dammit," I whistle as I grab his leash. He comes bounding off the couch and sprints across the living room floor to peek behind my legs, whimpering when he sees I'm alone.

It hurts all over again.

jensen

Kneeling down, I scratch the side of his head just under his ear and try to smile. "I'm sorry, boy. I know I told you this morning I was bringing her back, but it didn't work."

The little shit growls at me with his eyes narrowed.

"Hey. None of that. I tried, okay? I went to her work, I brought her a stupid flower, I told her everyone missed her. I tried."

Dammit puts his paw on my hand and pushes it down, glaring at me like he knows I used all the wrong words and tried to call it good enough.

Frustrated, I reach for his collar and attach the leash. "Fine. Be mad. I'm mad. We're all mad. But it's not gonna bring her back, okay? I failed, Dam. You're just gonna have to get over it, now c'mon."

That ninety-pound statue doesn't move when I stand and try to guide him toward the door. I tug a little harder on the leash to no avail.

"Seriously?"

He whines, tapping his front paws on the ground like he's trying to tell me something.

the night cap

"What?" I snap. "Let's go. Don't you wanna go for a walk?"

He barks loudly, standing up just to back up a few steps and sit down again.

"Walk, Dammit. Let's go."

Nothing.

"What, are you not understanding me? You seem to understand every other god-damn thing I don't say, so wh—"

It hits me like a ton of bricks.

Going back through the conversation I just had with Calliope, I realize I never once told her the thing she really needed to hear: that I miss her. I tried to pass the buck off on everyone else and failed to say the one thing that might prove to her things will be different. The one thing she could understand.

Son of a bitch.

"We'll talk about your attitude later," I mutter, unhooking his leash and hanging it back up as anxiety swirls in my chest. I can't pull my punches with her this time. I have to make it hurt. I can't protect myself anymore. "I'll be back, Dam. Daddy's gonna go get our girl… for real this time."

Chapter Sixteen: The Beginning

Callie

The moment I see him walk back inside Wrapz, my heart rate picks up again. It broke all over again earlier when he tried to pawn missing me off on anyone else.

I can't go back to giving all of me and getting so little in return. Clinging to the scraps he offered me only hurt me even more when he told me we could never be, and if he isn't to the point of being able to use his words, then I have to stay away.

But he's here again, sitting in a booth alone until my manager asks him to order food. I hide in the back while he orders and limit the time I spend up front after that, but by the time I'm clocking out and he's still dragging that burrito out even though it's been over an hour, I don't have any choice but to face him.

With my chin up, I waltz over to his table and stand over him, trying with all of me not to cry right there. I'm already hanging on by a thread after that flower. "What are you doing, Harv?"

"Eating," he says like it's obvious. "These are terrible burritos, by the way."

"I know. Okay then, enjoy your food. I'm gonna head home now."

I turn to leave, but his voice follows me and stops me dead. "Calliope, sit down."

I should walk away and protect myself, but my stupid feet don't seem to care about what I want them to do. Instead, I take a seat across from him and keep a respectable distance. "Still bossy, I see."

"Still calling me by that stupid nickname, I see," he retorts. "I need you to listen to me. Give me ten minutes of your time, and if you still want to walk away from me afterward, I won't stop you. Will you do that for me?"

jensen

Ten minutes. Then I'll be able to go cry for as long as I need to. "Okay."

He squirms like he has any right to be nervous here, then word vomits like he's just discovered language. "You're too good for me," he starts. "You know it, I know it, Daria knows it, the damn dog knows it. You're warm and smiley and optimistic, and I'm none of those things. I never have been, so it's not something I can blame on my ex. But I need you to somehow look past that for me. You make me crazy, Calliope. Your fashion choices are weird, you say dumb things, and you put woo girls to shame when you get too drunk. But you're so cute when you do it, it makes me nuts. Makes me literally fight people. Do you hear how insane that sounds? It's irrational and doesn't make a lick of fuckin' sense, but all I know is… my days suck without you."

My heart is racing so quickly as he speaks I feel my watch vibrate to tell me it's too fast, but I slip my hands under the table to hide it and swallow the lump in my throat. I can't cry, I won't cry. I keep watching him as he waits for me to say something, then continues when he realizes I won't.

"Not a day has gone by since the first night we met I haven't thought about you," he says quietly. "I tried to tell myself that it would stop, that I'd go back to my life like this never happened, and I can't. I'm an idiot. I'm worse than that, because I knew how backward I was being and did it anyway, cause sometimes the shit in my head gets me all twisted and nothing I say comes out right. It feels like a… a physical block that stops me from admitting how I feel. Call it a defense mechanism, call it a cop-out, whatever. I know it's not fair and I know I don't deserve for you to give me another chance, but… please?" His eyes soften, hands clenching on the table. "I want to be better for you. I'm crazy about you, sunshine."

I lose my fight. A tear slips out of my eye and slides down my cheek like a traitor, but I stop any others from escaping. I'm still speechless, but I know I need to say something to him because he's laying it all out on the table for me. "I never tried to change you," I finally whisper. "I tried to fit into your life as easily as possible, because I like you exactly as you are. Of course I had hoped you'd let me in with time, but don't think for one second you have to be anyone else to deserve me. I'm not too good for you. You're an amazing man, Harvey."

"So it's settled then," he says, standing up to throw away his trash. "You're coming back to work."

"Wait… to work?" I frown. I definitely thought he was asking me to be his girlfriend, but I must have read into something wrong and now I feel like an idiot. "No. I'm not."

Harvey chuckles, confusing me because it's such a rare sound. "Yes, you are. No girl of mine is gonna keep working a job she hates when there's an alternative. I'll just have to keep my grubby hands off you during business hours," he croons, helping me to my feet. "Is that a problem?"

I hate my brain in times like these because I need things laid out much plainer than a man like Harvey can do, but I let him pull me in. "And after business hours?"

the night cap

He exhales hard, kissing the top of my head as he wraps his arms around me. "I'll tie you to the bed so you can't leave or tap out on me, like a good boyfriend."

I melt into him, allowing a couple more tears to fall as his scent envelops me, and I know he can't see them. "I miss Red, Sam, Daria and Dammit too, by the way."

"Good, maybe they'll get off my back now," he grumbles, tugging my hair back so he can kiss the tears from my cheeks. "It's okay, pretty girl. You don't have to admit you missed me. Just promise me I won't have to miss you anymore."

I nod, letting him see how much I missed him too as my fingers curl into the back of his shirt. "Okay, boss man. I promise."

Cupping my chin, he kisses me gently. "Do you have everything? Purse, keys, whatever?"

"Yeah, it's all in my purse. I smell like cheap beans, though."

"You absolutely do, but I forgive you." He picks me up, glancing back over his shoulder at my manager standing behind the counter. "She quits, by the way. Again."

"What?!" he yells, moving to close the distance, but he stops a few feet away when he realizes how tall Harvey is. "Don't come crawling back this time, Callie. This is it. I don't care if you're willing to work the crap shifts. The answer is no."

My cheeks heat up at how quickly he called me out, embarrassment overtaking the anger with ease. "Whatever. Fine."

"She's not coming back anyway, bud. Your burritos suck." Harvey bends to pick my purse up and carries me outside, tipping his face up to look at me. "Kiss me before I go back in there and kick his ass for snapping at you."

I chuckle, knowing he absolutely will go back in there if I don't distract him, so I press my lips to his without hesitation and stay there, unable to pull away as he kisses me back.

It doesn't take long for it to turn heated, or for Harvey to growl, "Fuck," against my lips as his fingers squeeze my ass. "We're going home. Now."

the night cap

Yet he doesn't take me to my car, he takes me to his and drops me in the passenger seat, kissing me twice more before closing the door and hurrying around to get in.

"What about my car?" I ask breathlessly, already wet and practically begging him to drive.

"We'll come back for it." Harvey speeds toward his house, slipping his hand between my legs and squeezing. "Still haven't bought condoms."

"Harvey!" I growl. "Seriously? Why doesn't your bar have a vending machine or something?"

He eyes me. "Because I don't want to encourage drunk people to have sex," he explains. "But I wasn't telling you that as a way of saying we're not fucking. Just explaining why I'm not going to wear one when we do."

My legs clench tightly together, but his broad hand pushes them open again, making me fucking swoon. Before I can stop myself, I reach over and palm him greedily, making him grunt and struggle to keep his eyes on the road. "Don't stop," he growls, rutting up into my hand. "We're almost there."

The engine roars as he speeds up, and I listen like a good girl, leaning over to reach a little better as I kiss up his arm. "You want to fuck me, baby?"

"Yes." His voice is thick, deep, and his cock is rock hard under my hand. "Fuck. Sit back in your seat, sharp turn."

I barely have time to listen before he's jerking the wheel to the right, but a minute later we're pulling into the bar and he's rushing around to open my door again. His lips crash to mine as he picks me up and carries me not up the stairs to his apartment, but straight through the bar entrance to one of the tables. Shoving the upended chairs off, they clatter to the floor as he sets me down and kneels to tug my pants down, then lifts me up on the table and kisses me again.

I scramble to get him out of his jeans, his mouth instant and distracting on mine as I moan and tug, trying to get him free. It hits me then how real this is. He's really throwing all caution to the wind and taking me as his own. The emotions and vindication battling for dominance in

the night cap

my chest are almost too much, but the horny little beast inside me tells both feelings to get in the backseat so she can take the wheel. They listen, and I finally get his pants shoved down below his ass so that giant cock springs free.

Two thick fingers slide into my greedy pussy as his lips find my neck. "Come for me first, pretty girl. I don't want this to hurt."

Based on the size of him, I have a feeling it will anyway, but it's a pain I welcome — a pain I've longed for and dreamt about. Still, I know my gorgeous, grumpy man loves making me come, and I'll give him as many as he needs before he feels ready to fuck me.

My head falls back in pleasure as a loud, desperate moan leaves me, my hips rocking to meet that perfect hand while he fucks me with it. "Oh, Harvey!"

"Good girl, that's it. Fuck, I can't wait to feel your pussy squeeze my cock." His palm rocks forward, rubbing my clit as his other arm wraps around me to brace me. "Never giving you up again."

jensen

"Please!" I beg, coming hard a second later and clenching around those fingers so tightly, he groans.

"That's it, baby. Gush for me." His fingers slip out and spread my come all over my pussy, all over his cock, soaking us both as he slaps my clit with his length. "Lean back a little, baby. Spread those gorgeous legs for me."

I'm desperate not to disappoint him and instantly lay back, my thighs already trembling for what's coming. "Don't go easy on me," I gasp. "I'm yours."

"Are you?"

Slowly, he angles his cock down and slips inside of me, making me whimper so pathetically I blush. "Yes! Oh my god, you're so big."

"Breathe for me, Calliope. Let me in." Pulling out, he dips down to spit on my clit and sucks it into his mouth, then stands again to slide right back into me. "That's my girl."

I cry out, my legs tightening around him to pull him in. "I'm your girl," I moan. "Your good girl."

"Fuck." Grunting, he shudders as he bottoms out inside of me and leans down to kiss me. "Pussy's so fucking wet, pretty girl. Wrap those thick, beautiful thighs around me."

I do, squeezing him tightly to me as my fingers grip the back of his neck hard enough to leave nail marks. I feel so close to him in this moment my eyes water from happiness, and I kiss him back hard as he finally moves.

Thank god they bolted these tables to the ground. Each thrust gets rougher, faster, as he slips his hand between us to play with my clit. "Waited too long to be inside you, Callie."

"Me too," I admit. "When I saw you the second time we met, I wanted you to just take me. I was already yours, baby. God, I'm going to come again."

"I wanted to take you the first night," he admits, rubbing faster as his eyes darken. "Seeing you half naked in my bed almost—" he slams deep — "fucking—" again — "unraveled me."

I moan loud as I come for him, my entire body trembling as he fucks me better than anyone else ever has. "Harder!" I clench tightly around his cock as he loses rhythm, gripping my throat as he sucks

jensen

my bottom lip and his hips slap against my ass.

"Fuck, baby. I — stay still."

Harvey brutally fucks me as he hits his limit and tips over the edge, cock pulsing and pumping me full right in the middle of his bar.

I moan at the sensation, milking him for all he's got as he continues to roll into me and we ride that high together. No one's ever come inside of me before, and I feel so owned all I can do is smile. "That was… everything."

"No, baby," he argues gently, kissing my nose. "That was just the beginning."

Chapter Seventeen: The Game

Harvey

What the hell was I thinking hiring her back?

I was so close to everything I wanted, but I had to force her to tend bar for me again.

Big fucking mistake.

Her thick, perfect ass is all but hanging out of the skirt she's wearing tonight, and the fact that she's wearing a crop top is clearly just an attempt to fucking kill me. Every little peek I get at her belly is making my cock throb and my vision blur with the urge to bend her over and spank her until she's begging me to fuck her.

the night cap

And it's only getting worse.

"Aren't you cold?" I ask through gritted teeth. "I have a parka in the back you can borrow. Maybe a whole snowsuit."

She snorts, rising on her toes to kiss my cheek and ghost her hand along my crotch. "You're funny, Harvey. A parka?"

She turns away to help another customer, leaving me standing there with my fists clenched.

I need her. This is fucking torture.

Trying to behave, I stay busy in the back and in my office, but I'm greedy. I keep sneaking up front to see my beautiful girl and the way her hips are moving to songs I don't really know. Her lips move along with the words and her body moves in sync to the tune while she bartends her ass off.

The whole place has a better energy than it has in weeks, and I know I'd suffer a thousand boners I can't touch if it means I can keep her here with all of us.

She makes everything better.

As always, she spots me watching her and makes her way over, a mischievous grin on her face as she jumps into my arms and kisses me so everyone can see before wiggling back to her feet. "We need a new tap, handsome."

Shit.

"Calliope," I growl, nearly losing my mind at having her this close. "I thought we agreed I'd keep my hands to myself during business hours?"

"So keep your hands to yourself," she quips, running her fingers down my torso to grab my dick once again. "I made no promises about my hands."

Fuck, I want to test her. I want to walk her back to my office and lean against my desk as she uses her hands and that pretty little mouth, but we've got jobs to do. "You're bad."

"Maybe I need a spanking." She shrugs one shoulder and turns around, waving animatedly at Red and Sam when they enter.

It's the first time they've seen her since I got my shit together and begged her to come back, so I'm a little smug as they both reach across the bar to hug her and exchange excited greetings.

"See?" I gloat, coming up behind my beautiful girl to grip her hips and make sure she knows exactly how hard I am for her. "I told you I'd get her back. Neither of you believed me."

"Blink twice if you're in danger, love," Sammy whisper-yells. "No way you came back for the likes of him."

Callie laughs, pushing back against me happily as she looks up at me over her shoulder. "I came back for him," she admits. "But the only danger I'm in is the kind I like."

Oh, she's in danger, alright. My office locks and my patience is running thin.

I'm two seconds from slipping Daria a bonus to cover us when Callie squeals, scaring the shit out of me. I'm prepared to kill a spider, chase a mouse off, fight an asshole, something, but her eyes are on the guys who just walked in the door and she doesn't seem scared at all.

There are four of them, all ranging in height, and when she rushes over to hug them all, I wonder who the hell they are. The tallest one frowns over at me like he noticed how close we just were and I see him ask her who I am, making a blush coat her cheeks as she leads them over to me. "Harvey, these are my brothers: Giovanni —" she points at the second shortest one with a goatee first, who offers me a nod. "Leo —" this one is the shortest, his face smooth and frame thinner than the others, but he takes my hand with a knowing smile. "Adrian —" Even if she didn't tell me this was Adrian, I would have known. His eyes are already wandering around the bar like he's looking for someone to distract him, but his gaze snaps to mine when she says his name and he nods in greeting like Gio did. "And Xander." He's the tall one that seems to have a permanent frown on his scruffy face, and he takes my hand much tighter than Leo did.

"Harvey? Nice to finally meet you."

It doesn't sound like he means it very much, but Leo nudges him aside to lighten the mood. "Are you sure she should be bartending? She's clumsier than the rest of us combined."

Callie moves in to lean against me again and I drape an arm around her shoulders protectively, thanking god my jeans are thick enough to hide my rapidly fading boner. "She's one of the best bartenders I've ever had," I praise. "She's not as clumsy as you think."

the night cap

Three of them chuckle, but Xander, at least, smiles at her a little proudly. "Have you told him about the time you ran into that server and—"

"No. We don't have time for stories, Xan. Go sit and I'll bring you all your favorites."

She shoos them away and pulls me toward the bar, looking sheepish. "Sorry, I kinda told them I had a boyfriend and they insisted on coming in. They didn't say today, though, or I would have warned you."

The word 'boyfriend' still gives me weird, chaotic butterflies, like my nervous system is smart enough to be scared, but the rest of me knows she's worth it. "You absolutely would not have warned me because you know I'd have hid," I accuse playfully.

She grins cheekily and grabs my dick again, the bar blocking people from seeing, but I can feel her brothers watching us. Is she crazy? "No hiding now, baby. About that keg…"

She tosses her thumb toward it and clicks her tongue, turning away like she wasn't just bringing my boner back to life. Mentally, I decide to play a little game. The second this bar closes, she's going to come once for every time she touches me like that.

I hope she doesn't have plans in the morning.

Hurrying to the back, I tap the new keg and take a second to breathe, then wander back out to find her brothers all sitting at the bar laughing with her. She's distracted from her work, but she's smiling so widely that I can't bear to interrupt her. Instead, I rush to help Daria cover, and my girl sneaks away and stealthily grazes my dick again.

"Sorry, Harvey. Just needed to grab the cherries."

She moves back over to finish a drink as Adrian tries and fails to hit on the woman she's making it for, but I'm happy when he takes the rejection in stride and his siblings only tease him minimally.

At least none of them seem like creeps.

The girl looks back over her shoulder like she was hoping he wouldn't give up so easily, but his attention has moved on to his conversation with Callie and the chick has the nerve to mean mug her for it.

Chuckling, I move a little closer to her. "Playing hard to get doesn't work with that family."

"Why not?" she asks, glancing over at them again while tossing her hair. "Who even are they?"

Excellent fucking question. Sighing, I take it as a challenge to remember all of them by name, and I'm proud of myself when I do. "My girlfriend's brothers. Fun for me, isn't it?"

She laughs, looking at Callie a little lighter this time. "Yeah, looks like loads of fun for you. Sorry, dude. If you run, I won't blame you."

"Who, me?" I shake my head, gazing over at my gorgeous woman. "I've done my fair share of running in my life. She's finally given me a reason to stop."

The woman actually swoons in front of me. "That's the most romantic fucking thing I've ever heard. Jesus, and I can't even get a guy to look at me as I walk away. She sounds like a lucky girl."

"Nah, I'm the lucky one. But the whole point of me coming over here was to tell you I had to use words to make her understand I was interested. Go talk to Adrian. Maybe you'll have better luck being a little more direct," I offer.

She looks at him again just as he looks back over his shoulder at her, his smirk spelling trouble before he turns away again and she chews her lip. "Maybe. Thanks for the advice."

"It's on the house." It's a terrible joke I regret immediately, but most of my brainpower is currently being used to make sure I don't do something stupid. All four of her brothers are here. I can't just pick her up and carry her to my office.

... Can I?

Quirking an eyebrow, I sneak up behind her and slip my hand over her stomach, leaning in to whisper, "Drink some water, pretty girl. I need you hydrated tonight. You didn't think you'd get away with teasing me like this, did you?"

She whimpers, one hand reaching back to grip my shoulder as the other clenches on the bar. "Course not, baby." She pushes her ass back, then reaches to grab my dick again.

the night cap

"Oh, come on," Xander groans, but the other three laugh. "Cals."

Huffing, I wrap my hand around the front of her throat and meet his eyes as I kiss her cheek. "It was nice meeting you guys. Enjoy your night."

Turning on my heels, I make it back to my office to hide — and more importantly, plan.

My girl owes me a lot of orgasms.

Chapter Eighteen: The Belt

Callie

I'm already clenching my thighs as I lock up the bar, eager for what Harvey has planned for tonight's punishment. I saw the flames in his eyes all night. Even my brothers noticed the way he was looking at me, and I was relieved they were happy for me. Sure, Xander made a comment about how intense it was, but even he knows that's a good thing in a happy relationship, so he backed off when Adrian reminded him how possessive he gets with his girls.

Not that he's one to talk.

Saying goodbye to them is easier this time though, because I'm much more excited about this part of my night than I realized.

When Harvey walks out of his office, he's got his belt folded in his hand and a serene look on his face that tells me I'm in trouble. "Daria leave?"

Honestly, I don't have a clue. I wasn't thinking about anyone else. "Um… yes?" I bite my lip, knowing it only drives him crazier, and I'm not disappointed.

"Bend over the bar and pull your skirt up, pretty girl."

The noise that escapes me while I do as told is pathetic, but I never claimed not to be when it came to Harvey fucking Pierce. "Like this?"

"Mmhm. Just like that." Stepping behind me, I feel the edge of the leather gently grazing my skin as he explores my curves. "Do you know how many times you grabbed my dick tonight?"

"Um… twice?" I lie, wiggling a little in anticipation.

"Five," Harvey corrects. "Five times, Calliope. I'll give you a choice." Snapping the belt, he cracks it down on the bar next to me. "Five of these, or ten from my hand. Then I think I'll make you come that many times."

"Fuck me," I gasp, rocking back. "Belt. Please?"

"You got it, sunshine." His fingers slip into my waistband to pull my panties down, then rough fingers squeeze and lightly smack my ass to get my blood flowing. "Did you drink water?"

"Yes." I turn to watch him as much as I can. "I drank a few glasses."

He hums, spanking me a little harder with his bare hand. "Good girl. Just stay with me. Safety first."

A handful of spanks later, he's got that belt in his hand again and I'm so wet I feel it dripping down my thighs. "Harvey… show me I've been a bad girl."

The first upswing of that belt makes my ass jiggle on impact. "So fucking sexy," he praises. "Keep that skirt flipped up, baby. You're keeping it on tonight."

I groan, already struggling to catch my breath, and we've only just started. "This is as good as I imagined it would be."

Chuckling darkly, the second strike is harder. "For me too, baby. God, I love your body."

the night cap

The third and fourth come quickly, each harder than the last, and the crack that follows makes me jump. No impact comes with it, though. The fucker snapped it just to mess with me like my heartbeat isn't already trying to break records.

"Rude," I huff breathlessly, my toes curling in my shoes as I grip the bar top harder. "Baby."

It comes out like I'm begging, and maybe I am.

He lands the fifth one with a pleased groan and ducks down behind me, kissing the blazing hot skin before spreading my ass and slipping his tongue inside my pussy.

It's fucking heaven. Nothing has ever felt nearly as good as it does with him, and I have to fight the urge to tell him I'm falling for him. Or maybe I already fell, because I sure as fuck don't ever want to live without him again. "Harvey! I—"

I come so fast it catches me completely off guard, but he fucking loves it. Growling, "Good girl," he spreads my legs a little further and slaps my clit.

jensen

"There's one. You owe me at least four more, Calliope. Do it again."

His fingers pinch and rub my clit as his tongue licks over my abused ass, everywhere from the sensitive skin to my hole, and I give him two more in as many minutes. I always believed I was a one-orgasm-a-night kind of girl, but Harvey proves I'm not every time he touches me. It wasn't because I'm incapable of it. I was just never as stimulated by any other man in my life. This is about the strong connection we have, the trust, and the attraction. Plus… the man really knows what he's doing. "Please…"

I don't know what I'm begging for this time, but he does. He helps me stand up again and drags my shirt off, then undoes the clasp on my bra and peels it off my shoulders. I feel exposed like this, standing behind the bar wearing nothing but my skirt and my shoes, but the way his body presses against mine and his giant hands cup my tits reminds me I'm safe. "I think it's time I tease you," he rumbles, sneaking his fingers in my skirt to ghost over my pussy. "I was dying all night not being able to touch you just like this, so go on. Make me a drink, pretty girl."

I can hardly stand, but I reach out with shaking hands and grab him a cup. "W-What'll it be, Sir?"

"How about a Rob Roy? Let's see how much you remember from your first night here."

"One Bob Boy coming up," I joke, nerves creeping up my spine as I reach for the malt. "One and a half ounces… one ounce of sweet vermouth, um… a dash of bitters and a cherry?"

"Nope." Two fingers dip inside me, curling quickly and leaving my body too soon. "Try again."

"What did I get wrong?" I hiss, going back over the order in my head. "Wait, two dashes of bitters?"

His teeth sink into my shoulder as he bends me over and fingers me hard, not letting up this time until I'm screaming his name and just about to come for him again, then stops moving them but leaves them buried inside me. "Try again. Get it right and I'll let you come, baby."

jensen

I release a frustrated growl when it finally clicks. "Three! Three dashes. Baby, please!"

Harvey gives me three fingers this time for three dashes, reaching around to squeeze the sides of my throat. "Ride my fingers, pretty girl. Take it. Make yourself come."

"Thank you," I gasp, repeating it twice more as I bounce on his hand and work my way toward another one. "Everything you do feels so damn good."

"Yeah? Did you imagine doing this while you were working earlier? Driving me so fucking crazy that I bent you over and reminded you what happens when you're a brat to me?"

"Yes! Harvey!"

The tone, the words, all of him has me coming hard again, legs trembling as he works me through it, then holds his messy fingers to my lips. "Suck, Calliope."

I do it without question, moaning at the feeling of finally having his fingers in my mouth, and it's then I realize I'm going to have an entire secret relationship with these skilled hands. I'm falling for them too.

I mumble, "Please," around his fingers, drooling as he eases them back out over my tongue.

"Good girl. Can't wait to have that pretty mouth around my cock one day, but you still owe me one more. Here." Handing me a bottle of water from the cooler, he spins me around and lifts me up on the bar top. "Drink some of that for me. I'll wait."

Chugging it down, I use this time to catch my breath and stare at him. "You're so handsome. I can't wait to taste you too, baby."

He looks at me like I'm special, like he's never seen anything like me. "Lean back and get comfortable. I might not stop at one."

Placing a single kiss on my clit, he works two fingers inside of me and licks me slowly, deliberately. I learn quickly he wasn't lying when he pulls three more earth-shattering orgasms from me and I have tears falling down my face as I beg him to stop. "I can't! I can't have any more, Harvey."

jensen

His beard is shiny and soaked as he finally comes up for air. "You gave me seven, Calliope. That's perfect. Here." Tugging off his shirt, he slips it over my head and helps me back to my feet, snatching my bra, crop top, and panties off the floor. "You're staying with me tonight."

"Mmhm… I don't think I can walk. Will we ever make it to your bed, though?"

He snorts. "Thanks for reminding me. I don't take employees upstairs."

"Hey!" I pout, tapping him softly with the back of my hand. "I'm more than just your employee… right?"

The smile that spreads across his face is dazzling as he leans down to kiss me. "Yes, Calliope. So, so much more."

Spinning and bending down, he lets me climb on for a piggyback ride and takes me up the stairs, stopping just outside his door.

"Dammit's gonna maul you," he warns. "You ready?"

"Dammy! Yes!" I scramble off his back and push inside first, holding my arms out for the grumpiest pup in all the land. "I'm here!"

The giant Akita falls off the couch trying to get to me and bolts across the floor, knocking me down and trying to lick my face.

"Damnit, Dammit!" Harvey yells. "Off, boy. C'mon. Let her breathe."

He's too busy whimpering and wagging his tail so hard his whole body is shaking, and I think of how scared I was that I'd never see him again. He's here, I'm here, and it's obvious how much he missed me. "You give daddy a hard time for being a butt?"

He kisses me again, making me giggle as Harvey finally pulls him off. "Yes, he did. Little shit. But I need him to leave you alone for five minutes unless you plan on taking me to the hospital for blue balls."

"Oof, yeah, um… sorry boy. We need a little time before we cuddle, okay?"

I stand up and bite my lip at the bulge in his pants, grateful that Dammy doesn't fight Harvey too much as he leads him to his crate and locks him in. It's the first time I've ever seen the poor guy have to be in there, but he's got plenty of space and toys and blankets, and I've got a man to please.

"Come here," Harvey rasps, closing the distance between us and sweeping me into a messy, desperate kiss. I can still taste myself on his beard as he picks me up again and lays us down on the bed, and I curse the pants on his body.

"Off… take them off! Need you, baby. I'm still dripping for you."

He's frustrated as he gets up to strip, but it just makes it that much sweeter when he's crawling back up between my legs. "Are you sure, baby? You said downstairs you couldn't take anymore. I can do this myself just looking at you, if that's what you need."

"No… I want to feel you come inside me again," I admit. "I'm still not over that experience. Or you can have my mouth. You've been wanting it, haven't you?"

His lips trail over my calf as he lifts my legs to his shoulders. "I want all of you, Calliope. But I'm not going anywhere. We have time."

the night cap

The head of his cock slips up and down my messy pussy and he strokes it to get it wet, then eases inside me with a happy, low moan.

I don't think I'll ever get used to the feeling of this man stretching me. I clench around him before I take a deep breath to let him in, groaning as he bottoms out and rolls deep. "I already missed this and it's only been a day."

"Yeah? Maybe I won't make you wait a whole day next time," he chuckles, dropping down to kiss me slowly. "How much can you take, pretty girl? I don't want to hurt you, but I can still taste your pussy and I'm hanging on by a thread here."

His voice sends a shiver down my spine. "Give me all of you, baby. Don't hold back."

It feels like a loss when he pulls out of me, but his strong, expert hands roll me over and lift me up on all fours before I can protest. I get what he meant the second he slips back inside of me and grips my hips, because there's nothing gentle or reserved about the way he fucks me hard enough to send me jerking forward.

jensen

"Goddamn, Calliope. Stay put," he moans, wrapping a hand over my shoulder as the other wraps around the front of my thigh. "So fucking gorgeous. Pussy's so fucking hot and… wet… you sure you don't have one more for me?"

I do, I absolutely do, but I can't form the words to tell him that. Instead, I just let go. I fall into an oblivion I've never experienced before and moan his name like it's the only one I'll ever pray to.

Harvey's hips speed up as he praises me breathlessly and bottoms out again, pinning our bodies together as he finally gives me what I've been craving all night. I feel him pulsing inside of me, rocking his hips to make sure his come stays deep, and I make sure not to move away as he keeps us pressed together. A smile stays glued to my face until he finally lets me slump against the bed, and even then, it doesn't seem to be going anywhere. "That's so hot."

"Thank you for being you," he whispers, leaning down to kiss my shoulder and across my back. "You get one minute to relax and then I'll carry you to the bathroom."

the night cap

It's a sated, happy minute full of gentle touches and soft kisses, but he sticks to it. He helps me stand on my jelly legs as he cleans me, and by the time he's done, I feel strong enough to walk on my own — he just doesn't let me, and I love that he doesn't. He carries me back to bed and kisses me twice before going to take a shower himself, and I take that opportunity to let Dammit back out and make him jump on the bed to cuddle me.

I'm almost asleep when Harvey comes back in and freezes. "Oh, no. He's allowed on the couches, but not the bed. He's got his own. Down, boy."

Neither of us moves. My grip on his fur tightens a little, and the little shit plays asleep right alongside me.

"C'mon," Harvey pleads. "He sheds, baby. All over the blanket."

"Please?" I mumble sleepily. "Come cuddle us… I missed my guys so much."

I peek one eye open far enough to see him properly as he melts, shaking his head with a soft smile. "What are you doing to me, woman?"

"Loving you," I whisper. "Let me."

jensen

"Shit." The mattress dips as he climbs up and slots behind me, weaving one arm under my head and the other over me to rest on Dammit's stomach. "Guess this isn't so bad."

I hum, wiggling back with a soft smile on my face. "Not so bad at all."

As he settles in behind me, he gently presses his lips to the back of my head and whispers quietly, "I love you too, by the way. Thank you for not giving up on me."

Hearing those words feels so good I could cry, but instead… I close my eyes and let myself soak in them. I let myself actually believe them.

Harvey has fallen for me just like I have fallen for him, and instead of it being the scary thing we both feared, we'll catch each other and continue falling together. I'm not scared anymore. I know I don't have anything to fear while wrapped up in Harvey Pierce's arms, and I know he doesn't plan on letting me go ever again. It's a good thing too, because I don't plan on letting him go, either.

He's stuck with his sunshine.

Five Years Later: The Epilogue

Harvey

"Come here," I growl, pulling Calliope into a slow, heated kiss. She's being cagey tonight and I don't know why — we're throwing a wedding tomorrow, but it's not like we aren't already married. "What's wrong?"

"We're not supposed to sleep in the same bed," she whispers like someone might hear us. "It's tradition."

Blinking, I stick my finger in my ear and wiggle it. "Sorry, come again?"

Callie rolls her eyes at me, but there's a smile on her lips. She doesn't want to go anywhere any more than I want her to. "It's bad luck."

the night cap

"Maybe if we weren't already married," I argue. "We eloped to get away from all this bullshit. We're gonna be just fine."

Dammit's ancient ass comes around the corner dragging a silver duffle bag just as the doorbell rings.

"What the fuck is that?" I mutter. "Calliope Sofia Pierce, that better be a bag full of lingerie you're about to model for me, and if that isn't a pizza at the door, you and I are gonna have words."

"Well…" she trails off, drifting toward the door to open it and let Daria in. "Make those words quick, baby."

Oh, hell no.

"Out, Daria. If you think you're here to take her for the night, you're both high." I stand, snatching the bag from Dammit and slinging it over my shoulder. "She's staying here."

Rolling her eyes, Daria shuts the door behind her and steps into the foyer. We've had this house for a couple of years now and every time she comes over, she seems surprised I ever moved out of my upstairs apartment. "Don't be so *you* about this. Let the girl have her tra-

whole white-dress, black-tux wedding in the first place? To make her happy?"

God, I hate it when she opens her mouth and sense comes out. "Yes."

Calliope walks over to put a hand on my chest and stares into my eyes. "I don't want to sleep without you either, but it's tradition for a reason, right?"

I don't have it in me to point out that the "reasons" only include metaphors and surprises, which are two of my least favorite things. She just looks so happy and hopeful that I can't bring myself to ruin it for her.

Folding my hand over hers, I frown down at her. "You sure this is really what you want?"

"No," she admits. "I don't think I'll ever sleep good without you next to me. I guess I just feel like it's something my mom would make me do if she was still around."

Goddamnit. Cupping her chin, I kiss her slowly. "Okay, sunshine. You can have your tradition. I waited years for you to turn up in my life. I guess I can survive one night without you. But I have a condition, though."

the night cap

"Anything." Her eyes are filled with so much devotion, I believe her. She'd do anything for me if it was in her power.

Good.

"I get you first." Turning to Daria, I nod toward the door. "Go home. I'll bring her to you tonight when I've had my fill of her."

"So… never then?" she quips, crossing her arms. "I'm supposed to believe you'll really bring her?"

"Yes. You know better than anyone the lengths I'll go to in order to make her happy. This is what she wants, so I'll have her to you before midnight."

Her eyes snap to Callie. "You good with this?"

She nods, pulling that bottom lip between her teeth to drive me crazy as she smiles. "I'll be there in a bit, Daria. My brothers will be here around then anyway for his bachelor night."

"Excuse me?" I twitch, curling my hand around the back of her neck. "Do you want to run that by me again?"

"Not really." I hear the door click as Daria takes that as her cue to leave, and my gorgeous wife drops to her knees to distract me. She pulls my cock out, eyes filled with mischief as she strokes and then rushes out, "Red and Sam too," before sucking me in.

God-fucking-damnit, those are *not* the people I want to be thinking about right now. "Calliope," I growl, fisting a hand in her hair to halfheartedly tug her off.

The feral little growl she releases has me pausing and letting her take me deeper, one hand wrapped around the base as the other reaches to massage my balls.

When her gaze flicks to mine again, I lose all desire to make her stop. If she wants to distract me… maybe I'll let her.

"Open, pretty girl. Let me in that infuriating little throat."

She smiles around me, moving her hand so she can take me to the hilt, and when it drops down to slip into her leggings, I wish I had a better fucking angle.

One particularly skillful suck has my legs locking and everything else fading. "Fuck. That's it… good girl. Rub your clit, baby. Make yourself come."

Her moan vibrates down my cock, her gorgeous hazel eyes rolling as she lets pleasure take over everything and I fuck her throat even deeper.

It's a struggle to hold back enough so I can see what she's doing, see how close she is to coming. Slowing down, I keep my cock buried and only pull back enough to let her breathe through her nose each time, teasing us both until I've all but forgotten that I didn't want to come like this.

The night is still young.

"Close yet, baby?" I whisper, pulling out to smack her wet, swollen lips and let her speak. "Let me see your fingers."

She pulls them out with a nod, showing me how wet and shiny they are before sucking them into her mouth.

Feeling robbed, I drop down to finger her myself, eye level with her. "Did I say you could have that?"

She shakes her head, a smile dancing across her lips as another moan escapes them. "No, Harvey."

I'll never, ever get used to the way it feels when she says my name like that.

"Mmhm. Come for me, pretty girl. Soak my fingers and then I'll let you finish what you were doing. Need to know my wife is taken care of first."

"You always take care of me, baby. Oh fu—"

She groans, hips moving to ride my hand as she gets more desperate by the second, and I catch her in a messy kiss as I feel her pussy clench. "There it is. Breathe, pretty girl. I want fucking all of it."

Callie gasps into my mouth, then latches onto my bottom lip as she comes hard and gives me exactly what I want. Slowly, carefully, I ease my hand out of her leggings so I don't waste a drop, then hold her head to keep her close to me as I lick my fingers clean. The taste of her makes my cock throb violently, her hand wrapping around it a second later as she leans in to inhale my scent.

"I love you," she whispers. "I love all of you with all of me."

This is *absolutely fucking not* how I planned on getting off the night before our second wedding, but I'm too far gone to ask her to stop. Not when she says things like that and means it the way she does. My chest caves in on itself as

the night cap

my hips buck and all I can do is hold her close and whisper back, "I love you more."

A final twist of her hand has my balls tightening and my breath catching, and my perfect girl wiggles down instantly to suck me in and catch every single drop on her tongue.

God, she turns me into putty.

Petting her head, I brush her hair over her shoulder to see her face. "I mean it, Calliope. Maybe I say it enough, maybe I don't, but I love you. Enough that I'll keep your punishments for tonight to a minimum when we get to our honeymoon."

Callie pulls off and wipes her mouth with the back of her hand, but I can see she's barely hiding a smile. "Punishments? Plural?"

"Mmhm. One for leaving me tonight and one for each of the people you invited here," I explain, gripping her chin to kiss her. "I love you and I'm not mad, but I'm still going to edge you for it until you cry."

She hums, kissing me again with that mischievous look. "Can my brothers count at one?" she bargains as if she doesn't love every punishment I've ever given her. "It's not my fault there's four of them."

It's almost embarrassing how quickly I cave. "Fine. But Red and Sammy still count as two, so you're still ending up with four."

"Okay." She looks like she just won something with that, but before I can say anything back, our door is flying open and her brothers are walking in.

"Gross," Xan yells, but Adrian whistles at my bare ass before I can pull my pants back up.

"Guys!" Callie yells, looking flushed as all hell. "Have you ever heard of knocking?"

Leo shoves the two younger ones softly. "I told them to wait. Daria was nice enough to warn us."

"I did," she confirms, stepping in behind them. "Loudly and vehemently, but they don't listen. Sorry, boss."

Rubbing my face, I glare at my wife and future bride. "Baby," I mumble. "Why do you hate me?"

the night cap

"I don't," she pouts, leaning in to kiss me. "They hate us."

"Ehh, we love you both. You more, of course, but... Harvey by default," Adrian says, earning a stiff middle finger from his sister as he opens up a snack like he's relaxing at home. "You two need to go, though. Strippers will be here any minute."

That gets my girl's attention and she rounds on them like a little demon crawling out of hell. "The what?"

"The *strip-pers*," Giovanni enunciates slowly. "You told us Harvey wouldn't leave his house for some stupid bachelor party, so we're bringing the bachelor party here."

Leo smacks his shoulder. "Don't do that to her. He's kidding," he promises. "Just some whiskey and good friends."

"I don't care either way," she lies, crossing her arms and looking half-tempted to slap all four of them. "I'm not a jealous person."

They all laugh at her, Daria included, and she spins back toward me with a frown. "I hate them all."

jensen

"You invited them," I remind her darkly. I've grown to love her brothers too, but not tonight. Not when all I want is to get lost in the luscious curves of my wife's body and forget the fact that she's making me put on a show tomorrow. I hate being the center of attention, hate people watching me. Yet for her... I'd do just about anything.

"Someone call for whiskey?" Sam yells, and I realize with a deep sigh that I can't kick all of them out just to suffocate myself between Callie's thighs.

Well, I *can*... but something tells me I'd be the one being punished then. "Come on in, Sammy. Red with you?"

"Oh, he'll be along in a moment. He brought a char-coot-ee board, whatever that is. You want this in the kitchen?" Holding up a bag full of whiskey bottles, Callie's brothers take notice and guide him to the right spot, following him.

Daria tells Callie she'll be in the car then ducks out, and finally, for one moment, I have my girl to myself.

"Every time Adrian says something questionable, I'm taking a shot. If I'm too drunk to walk tomorrow, just re-member whose fault this is."

"No... don't play that game. You'll die!" Panic overtakes her beautiful fea-tures as she glances at her hot mess of a brother. "I'll glue his mouth shut, how about that? Or a staple gun might work."

So, so fucking beautiful. "How did I get so lucky?" I ask gently, pulling her at-tention back to me. "I won't be drinking tonight, baby. If you need me for any reason, no matter what time it is, you call me. Do you understand?"

She smiles, staring up at me with so much love in her eyes, I melt. "I will, Harvey. But don't worry about me. Have some drinks so you survive the night with these assholes. I'll miss you, but I'll be okay, and I can't wait to marry you again. The rest of our life begins tomor-row, big guy."

Shaking my head, I bend down to kiss her nose. "Calliope, my life began again the day you first set foot in my bar. I never thought I'd get a chance to be happy, and you proved to me in a fort-night that I had no idea what true happi-ness really looked like. So call me, don't

jensen

call me. Marry me twice or a hundred times. I'm all yours, and I'd move Hell itself to see you smile."

I kiss her fully before she can point out that I'm not supposed to give my vows until tomorrow. If she thinks that was good, she hasn't seen anything yet.

I'm only just getting started.

Also By Octavia Jensen

BOYS OF BRISLEY:
King Hunt
Exposed King

ELEVEN:
11 Hours//11 Scenes//11 Dates
Sin Sessions
Invite Only
Handle Me

WHITECREST:
Business & Pleasure
Eyes On Me
Can't You See
Over A Cliff
Motocross My Heart
Rose-Colored Boy
Time for a Wedding

BURNING RIVER:
Santa's Lay
All Over You
Heels Over Head
Just Like This

STANDALONES:
Don't Go
With All My Broken Pieces
Second Chance Christmas

BLACKRIDGE:
Take Me Twice

DOMINGO:
Onside Kiss

Visit Octavia Jensen

www.octaviajensen.com

Facebook: Author Octavia Jensen
Instagram: @authoroctaviajensen
TikTok: @authoroctavtiajensen

Printed in Great Britain
by Amazon

25711830R00121